THE ROAD

—— *to* ——

REVELATION

The Beginning

THE ROAD

—— *to* ——

REVELATION

The Beginning

Clifford T. Wellman Jr.

Published by Hidden Lodge, LLC.

www.TheRoadToRevelation.com
www.CliffWellman.com
www.facebook.com/TheRoadToRev
www.facebook.com/CliffWellmanAuthor
www.twitter.com/RoadRevelation
RoadToRevelation13@gmail.com

Book design copyright © 2016, 2021 by Clifford T. Wellman Jr. All rights reserved.
Cover design by Clifford T. Wellman Jr. & Brandi Doane McCann.
Cover photo by Brandi Doane McCann
Interior design by Clifford T. Wellman Jr.

Published in the United States of America

ISBN: 979-870026-273-6   (hardcover)
ISBN: 978-198034-483-4   (paperback)
Kindle: ASIN: B08L71JG7T   (kindle)

1. Fiction / Christian / Futuristic
2. Fiction / Thrillers / General

DEDICATION

To my father.

Thank you for always being there for me.

Thank you for showing me how to love.

Thank you for showing me what it means to be a man.

Know always that you are loved.

OTHER BOOKS BY

Clifford T. Wellman Jr.

The Road to Revelation Series:

#1 – The Beginning

#2 – World at War

#3 – Darkness Falls

#4 – Life & Death

#5 – Dire Warnings

#6 – Day of the Lord (Coming 2022)

Real Estate and Investing:

- How I Retired By Age 45

Acknowledgments

I would like to thank Jesus Christ, my God and my savior. Without you, I would not have been able to share this story.

Philippians 4:13 - "I can do everything through him who gives me strength."

I would also like to thank my friends and family for the support and love that they have given me throughout this journey. For those of you who shared my excitement in writing this book, your excitement helped keep me going.

Thank you to my wife, who spent hours reading and editing. I had pages and pages of edits and changes. I could not have done it without you.

PROLOGUE

Almost forty five years ago

I t was a moonless night when the nameless woman gave birth to a son. She had been shunned by her family and friends because she conceived out of wedlock. She was the oldest of six children and lived all her life in the city of Istanbul, Turkey. She was a faithful Muslim, but there had been one night almost, nine months before, when she lost control of her body. She had a vague recollection of the night and actually woke up the next morning believing it had been a dream. In the dream, she had been attacked by a demon who lay with her. She struggled to fend him off, but he had been too strong and had his way with her. Her body ached where the demon had touched her, but she knew that it could not have been real. However, in the following days and months, she began to show signs that she was carrying a baby.

She attempted to hide the pregnancy, but after six months, that became impossible. She finally confessed to her mother and father that she believed that she was pregnant. Her father's anger was explosive, and the force of his blow to her face was extreme. As she lay on the floor, she could see the pain in his eyes and the suffering in her mother's eyes as well. Her mother would do nothing to stop her father from delivering more punishment, but as her father made a move to grab her by the hair, he grabbed his chest instead.

The woman could still recall the sight of her father dying beside her on the floor and her mother screaming in sorrow next to him. Even the pain of childbirth couldn't hold back the sorrowful memory of her parents that day. That day, she immediately knew that her life would never be the same and decided to leave her family. She ran away that night and would never come back. As she left her house, she turned and saw her younger brother looking out of the window. She waved, and he waved back. Then she turned and ran, knowing that she would never see any of them again.

The sound of her son's first cry made her smile. While the nurse cleaned the child, she felt the first wave of pain. Instinctively, she grabbed her stomach. A moment later, the pain was so unbearable that she let out a violent scream. The nurse rushed the child out of the room as the doctor attended to her.

"Help me!" the woman screamed.

The doctor's reaction was one of compassion and knowing. He placed one hand in hers and the other on her forehead. A moment later, the room began to fade, and soon she would see no more. In the other room, the nurse held out the baby to an older couple who had been unable to have children. This child was a blessing to them.

"Allahu Akbar!" the man said as he held his son for the first time. His wife smiled as she caressed the child's cheek.

The boy would someday grow to be a powerful man. He would receive the best education and would be given everything.

I watched as the Lamb opened the
first of the seven seals. Then I
heard one of the four living
creatures say in a voice like
thunder, "Come!" I looked, and
there before me was a white horse!
Its rider held a bow, and he was
given a crown, and he rode out as
a conqueror bent on conquest.
— Revelation 6:1–2

CHAPTER 1

Ford – Present Day

The sun was creeping over the horizon as the world in front of him began to awaken. The tips of the trees were set ablaze as last night's frost began to melt. A few minutes ago, the world was dark, and the stars were bright. The constellations had been alive like only they could be in Northern Michigan. It always amazed Ford how the scene in front of him changed with the ever-increasing light of the rising sun.

Ford had been sitting in this ladder stand since 6:00 a.m., waiting for a world-class buck to saunter by. His many trail cameras had provided glimpses of the monster that ruled these woods. As far as he could tell, the deer had at least sixteen points and probably ran about 250 pounds. Only in Northern Michigan did deer like this exist. Ford had some good luck hunting here since he had purchased the property a few years ago, but never had he witnessed a deer as magnificent as the one that he called *the beast*.

The shadows danced and teased as the sun shed more light on the terrain. During this hour, you could never be sure what you saw until it was right under your nose. It was about a minute after shooting time when Ford saw him come out of the woods. Actually, he heard him first. Big bucks tend to make a lot of noise as they work their way through the narrow trails. The buck walked up the trail that Ford had cut earlier that summer. The buck was following the trail with his nose down to the ground, sniffing the scent of a doe that had passed by only a few moments earlier. Ford had considered shooting the doe, but he knew that there was a buck following her. You could tell it in the way that she moved. She knew that a buck had been trailing her.

At twenty feet above the ground, there was no way that this buck would see him unless Ford made some overt move. He kept himself still and waited for the beast to come into range. It only took fifteen minutes, but to Ford, it felt like a lifetime before the deer made it to the bait pile, which was about thirty yards from his ladder stand. The deer stopped to eat the carrots that Ford had placed there last evening, but it was facing Ford, and he didn't have a good shot on the beast yet. Twice, Ford had counted to himself the number of points that the beast had among his antlers. Sixteen had been the count both times. Ford had never before seen a deer like this, and he could feel his heart racing. He was just waiting for that moment when the deer would turn broadside.

Yesterday had been different. As usual, Ford had gotten up early; and on his walk out to the ladder stand, he realized that the moon was gone. Just the day before that, the moon had been a small sliver of light, and the deep red and orange of the sunrise engulfed the small slivered moon. Knowing that it had been a new moon didn't help the unnerving feeling the empty sky left in him. Ford hoped that tomorrow he would see the moon again. But more unnerving was the sudden appearance of the fog. It seemed to come down from the heavens to obscure everything. The world seemed to go quiet once the fog was complete, and then there was a shudder.

Ford had always been in tune with the spiritual world. Prior to becoming a Christian, he had explored many Native American cultures. He had learned to be close to the earth. Those skills had never left him, and he could feel the combined energies of the world. The shudder had been an omen, and Ford was soon to discover what it meant. Out in the woods, he never really knew what was going on out in the world, and that was the way he liked it. But that day, Ford knew that he would have to come out of the woods and get back to civilization to see what was going on. Jesus told his disciples that there would be wars and rumors of wars and that these were the beginnings of the birth pains. By birth pains, he meant the worldly problems that would occur during the seven-year tribulation.

Ford had been studying biblical end-times prophecy for several years. It had been this study that finally led him to Jesus. You could say that the end-times had scared the hell out of him. According to his study, the next major event that would signal the coming of Jesus was the conquest of the Middle East by Iran. The current US president had made it very easy for Iran to advance its positions throughout the Middle East. Iran now had influence throughout the region, and it had become emboldened. It is funny, all the things that can go through a hunter's mind while waiting for a deer to get into position. After another ten minutes or so, the beast presented himself for a nice broadside shot. Ford slowly raised his crossbow and switched off the safety. He took a deep breath and slowly squeezed the trigger.

CHAPTER 2

Samantha

Samantha grew up in a small town in Michigan, but her life had taken her all the way to New Mexico. Samantha or Sam, as her friends called her—missed her hometown, but she sure enjoyed the warm New Mexico winters. By all accounts, the beginning of November wasn't really winter, but soon the season would change. No one could have foreseen the events that were about to occur. Well, that isn't entirely true. They were foretold a long time ago but had been forgotten by most people these days.

Sam was sitting on the porch of their modest three-bedroom home when her phone rang. She lived with her husband and her two sons on a nice twenty-acre plot of land that was on the outskirts of town. The New Mexico desert stretched out in front of her, and a small mountain range plastered the horizon. Michigan enjoyed some amazing sunsets, but for her, nothing could beat the view that she had right now.

"Hello," Sam said. It was her mother. Her mother and father lived back in her hometown in Michigan. "Hey, Mom, how are you doing?" she asked.

"We're doing fine. Your father is out shoveling off the drive," Sam's mother answered. Her father was close to seventy years of age and probably shouldn't be shoveling the driveway, but no one could tell him what to do. If he had it in his mind to do something, he was definitely going to do it.

"I hope he is taking it easy," Sam said. She was always concerned about her father overexerting himself these days. "You know how your father is," Sam's mother started.

"He doesn't listen very well." Sam's mother sighed.

"Okay, well, keep an eye on him, Mom," Sam exclaimed.

"So how are you feeling, Mom?" Sam asked.

"Honey, I'm fine," her mother answered. "My hip is still a little sore, but it's getting better. It hasn't slowed me down too much," she added with a smile. She had fallen the other day and bruised her hip. Thankfully, she didn't break anything. Sam's mother was always upbeat and positive. Sam had gotten her optimism and mental toughness from her mother.

"How much snow do you have?" Sam asked. *I'm sure glad I still don't live there*, she thought. "We probably got two inches last night, but overall, somewhere around six inches. So it hasn't been too bad yet," her mother replied. There was a pause that seemed unnatural to Sam. She had always been able to freely talk with her mother, and it almost frightened her that they were discussing the weather.

"So what's up, Mom?" Sam asked. Again, there was a pause. Something was definitely bugging her mother.

"Sam, I'm really not sure," her mother started. "Maybe I just miss you, but I've been worried about you a lot lately."

"Oh, Mom, you don't need to worry about us," Sam reassuringly said. "We are all doing just fine here. We are definitely staying warmer than you two," she jokingly said.

Sam decided to change the topic a bit and asked about her brother. Sam's brother Brian was sort of the black sheep of the family. He wasn't a bad guy, but he just seemed lost. Sam had always worried that he still wasn't saved yet. The last she knew, Brian still wasn't attending a church. He was younger by almost ten years and still lived at home. In his early thirties, he still couldn't get it together.

"Mom, how is Brian doing?" Sam asked. She knew that she should call him herself, but he never seemed to want to talk much, and it broke her heart that things were so distant between them.

"Oh, he's fine," her mother answered. "He has a new girlfriend. She seems nice, but I don't know much about her."

"A girlfriend, huh?" Sam questioned.

"Yes, she's a little younger, I think in her mid-twenties. It sounds like she has a pretty good job here in town, but she also has a child," her mother reported. "I think she teaches third grade."

"Wow, Brian and kids," Sam exclaimed. "How long have they been going out?" Sam questioned.

"I think Brian said that it has been over six months," her mother answered.

For Brian, having a long-term relationship was very rare. Six months was probably the longest that he had ever dated someone.

"Do you know if they go to church?" Sam asked. She knew that this could be a touchy subject with her mother. Her mother was a devout Catholic and had raised all her five children to go to church.

Sam still attended a church but was no longer Catholic. She and her mother had gotten into a fight about it when she told her mother, but in the end, her mother was just happy that she was still attending a Christian church. Sam's older brother Ralph had moved into Michigan's Upper Peninsula and was still a practicing Catholic. Her two younger sisters were both married in the Catholic Church. Rebecca was the third oldest behind Ralph and Sam. She had married a man from Ohio who didn't attend church very often. Rebecca still went every Sunday and took her three children, but it put a strain on their marriage because he wasn't a strong believer. Sam was closest with Rebecca, and Sam knew that she was saved. Sonia, the second youngest, was five years younger than Sam, so they were not as close. She had been the wild one of the family; but after college, she met her husband, who was a devout Catholic, and she settled down. Sam's mother just loved Sonia's husband. Sonia and her husband had six children, and they only lived a few miles from Sam's parents. It made Sam's mother very happy, being able to see some of her grandchildren once in a while. It made Sam want to go back home with the boys.

"I'm not sure if they go to church," her mother answered.

"I don't see them on Sundays, and I'm not sure if she's Catholic or not." Her mother continued. "I try not to bug Brian too much about it anymore. I'm just too tired of fighting with him about it."

Sam decided that she would call Brian tomorrow and talk to him. It had been far too long since they had talked. With Christmas around the corner, she decided that she would call all her siblings.

"Honey?" her mother asked.

"Yes, Mom?" Sam answered. There was a pause again. Sam knew that something was going on that her mother didn't want to talk about.

"Please be careful, dear," her mother said. "I love you very much, sweetie!"

"I love you too, Mom!"

"I will let you get back to whatever you were doing. Tell Rob and the boys that we love them!"

"I will, Mom. Give Dad a big hug for me and tell him that I love him too," Sam said. "And don't let him work too hard," she added.

"Good-bye, dear!" her mother said.

"Good-bye, Mom."

Sam hung up the phone and wondered what was troubling her mother. She was concerned that her mother had been so silent. She hoped that nothing was wrong with her father.

Back in Michigan, Sam's mother hung up the phone and thought about the dream that she had the previous night. She had been having the same dream for weeks, and she was beginning to lose sleep over it. Then, a night ago, she had the dream about Sam.

CHAPTER 3

Ford

After field dressing the beast, Ford began making his way back to the lodge. He would need help putting him on the 4×4, and he hoped that his son, Tom, was home. This property was the place that he called home for the last few years. Ford had finally been able to buy the land that he had always wanted. He found a great deal on two hundred acres. It was mostly wooded with some wetlands. There was a small river and a couple of ponds. The house wasn't anything special, but it was nice enough and somewhat unique. There were two pole barns and a henhouse. It had everything that they needed. They had been working to make the property as close to off the grid as possible. On his way back home, he said a quick prayer of thanks to God for the great harvest of the buck that he had just shot.

When he arrived home, he yelled into the house for Tom, "Hey, Tom, can you give me a hand?"

"Sure, Dad! Just a second," Tom replied.

"Meet me in the barn!" Ford yelled back.

Tom had graduated from college this past spring and was still looking for a job. So in the meantime, he stayed with them, and surprisingly, he helped out quite a bit. Ford and Tom had almost killed each other before Tom went away to college. It was the typical power-struggle stuff that came with teenagers. Fortunately, all the arguments had never really harmed the great relationship that they shared.

Throughout the years, as a family, they had taken seriously the reality that they would most likely witness the coming seven-year tribulation. Ford knew that there would be trials before those seven years, and he had done his best to prepare his family for them.

"Hey, Dad, what's up?" Tom asked.

"Well, I have to show you something," Ford said with a smile.

Tom looked at him a bit weird, and as they climbed aboard the 4×4 and started down the camp trail, the light bulb in his head went off. Tom turned to his father with a huge grin and yelled, "Nooo!"

Ford continued to drive and just let his smile tell the whole story.

When they arrived at the location where Ford left the beast, Tom was ecstatic.

"Oh my gosh! He's so huge!"Tom yelled. He turned and gave his dad a serious fist bump.

The two of them were all smiles as they loaded the massive buck onto the 4×4 and began driving their harvest back to the pole barn.

After hanging the deer in the barn and washing up, Ford sat down in front of the television to check out the news. The shudder that he felt the day before was still on his mind. He turned on Fox News only to discover that nothing new was happening. He realized then that he would have to dig deeper into the Internet to find out what was going on. There were other news sources outside the mainstream media that generally told a better version of the truth. Ford decided that it was time to do a little research.

CHAPTER 4

Samantha

When Sam hung up the phone with her mother, she said a prayer. She asked God to watch over her mother and father and to protect them. She asked that Brian find a path to God. She asked God to protect the rest of her siblings and their families.

When she was done praying, she opened her eyes and looked up. Her eyes immediately gravitated to the horizon and to the mountains. Sam was a dreamer and a hopeless romantic. She saw the horizon as a symbolic representation of mankind's potential future. The possibilities were limitless to Sam.

Today, however, she had a sense of gloom as she looked at the horizon. The mountains were clothed in dark clouds, and the sky was beginning to change to a strange shade of green. Prior to the phone call with her mother, everything had seemed normal, but now the sky was making a turn for the worse.

In Michigan, this color of green in the air would have immediately made her think that a tornado was imminent. Tornados were very rare in New Mexico and almost seemed impossible, but Sam decided that she would go check the Weather Channel to see what was going on.

Sam walked into the living room to find her husband, Rob, flipping channels and enjoying a beer. He had just gotten home from a long day's work, and he needed a little time to unwind. Watching TV and drinking a beer wasn't his normal unwind routine. Normally he would do something that required activity, maybe fiddle with something in the garage or in the yard.

Sam looked at him questioningly and said, "How was your day?" as she walked over and gave him a quick kiss.

"Well, uh, it was okay. Nothing special, I guess. I just have been in a funk all day," Rob said, then paused. "So I decided that I would just have a beer and relax a bit. Want to join me?" he continued with a smile.

"Sure, but first I was hoping to check the Weather Channel really quick. It looks like a storm is brewing, and I hope that it isn't too bad."

"Okay, we can do that," he replied as he changed the channel.

They watched with interest for about ten minutes before they came to the conclusion that nothing menacing was coming. Sam went to the kitchen to grab a drink. She decided on ice water; for some reason, she didn't want a beer. As she was filling her glass, she looked out the back window and noticed that the clouds had almost cleared up. She frowned to herself, wondering what was going on.

CHAPTER 5

Ford

Ford had been sitting at the computer for a couple of hours before his wife, Abby, came into his office.

"Hey, sweetie, are you going to play with that thing all night?" she said with a sly smile.

"Huh? Uh, no, sorry, I just got enthralled in my latest research," Ford replied.

He had started out scanning his normal news websites to see if anyone recognized any strangeness in the world. After about twenty minutes, he concluded that nothing overt was going on, and he decided that he would continue some research he was doing on the book of Revelation, specifically having to do with the seven seals found in chapter 6.

"So what are you discovering now?" Abby playfully said.

Ford thought to himself that Abby must have had a really good day, and he smiled. "Well, do you recall when I told you that I thought that the first seal had already been opened?" he asked.

"Sure," she replied, her smile diminishing a bit. She realized that Ford was deep into his research, and it was going to be tough to make him more playful.

"Well, I think that we are on the verge of the second seal being opened. Do you remember the book I read that outlined some of the common themes in Revelation and Daniel?" he continued.

Abby nodded. She knew that he was getting very excited about his work, and she started to smile again. Ford had opened her eyes to so many things that were going on in this world and how they most likely were related to the soon-to-be second coming of Jesus. She loved his enthusiasm for his work and for his family. Once he had found Jesus, he had become a far better husband and father. Not that he was bad before, but now he was just more caring and loving. She loved that about him.

"I believe that Iran will soon begin the conquest of the Middle East, and no one will stop them. Even the United States won't do anything. I've discovered links between Daniel, Ezekiel, Isaiah, and Revelation. The prophecy in all these books seems to be pointing to the events that will occur prior to the coming of Christ!" Ford explained with so much excitement that Abby just couldn't help but smile.

"I'm finishing up some notes, and then I'll be done. Fifteen minutes tops," Ford stated.

Abby nodded and smiled. She came up to him and kissed him gently on the cheek. He smiled and went back to his work.

Fifteen minutes later, Ford emerged from his office. He was right on time for a change. He walked into the living room and sat down next to Abby on the couch. He gently kissed her on the forehead and grasped her hand. The boys were watching some documentary on the History Channel, and as usual, they were debating various points in the presentation. Abby and Ford always enjoyed their playful banter. He dearly loved them all, and he wanted to find the answers in time to help them all through the tough times ahead.

John, their youngest, was a senior in high school. He and Tom were close even though almost five years separated them in age. Ford could tell that John was happy to have Tom around after four years of being an "only child." At least he had someone to share in the daily chores.

As Ford listened and watched his family, he could feel his heart breaking. Trouble was coming, and he knew that he could never be prepared enough. He knew that soon this life would never be as easy as it was today.

CHAPTER 6

Nigel

It was midnight, and Nigel was heading south on I-69 toward Indianapolis. There was little traffic at this hour, so he wasn't concerned about exceeding the speed limit. But given his cargo, he decided not to push it too far. The lights of the city had already appeared on the horizon, but darkness seemed to engulf him. He was doing the will of Allah, but for some reason, he had begun questioning himself. As he approached the interchange that would take him to I-65, he whispered, "Allahu Akbar," which means "God is great," in hopes of improving his mood. Soon he would be on the freeway that would take him toward his final destination.

Weeks before, his team had stolen the van, had it repainted, and gave it new license plates. Only under close inspection would anyone know the nature of this vehicle. It was a white cargo van with no rear windows. It had been painted with the logo of a popular cable company, and each of his crew had been outfitted with the proper uniform. They had the proper credentials and should have no problem reaching their target.

The van left Detroit around 8:00 p.m. under the cover of night and should arrive at its destination around 5:30 a.m.

This would give them more than enough time to get in place for the big event.

Nigel was the leader of this small crew of four. As he drove, he wondered about each of them. He knew very little about them but knew enough to recognize that they had the skills to complete their task. Ali Basharat, the leader of their group, had told him that Nigel and his team would be the tip of the sword. He said that Nigel's team was one of the many teams that would coordinate their attacks and, God willing, would eventually bring America to its knees.

Saif was in the passenger seat, listening to some music from his native country of Syria. Saif was illegally in the country. He had come into the United States through Mexico near Laredo, Texas. It had taken him almost a year to get from Damascus to the compound where Nigel had met him. The civil war that wreaked havoc on his country had already displaced half of his population. Saif believed that America was at fault for not stopping the Syrian president from continuing to unnecessarily punish the Syrian people. He wanted vengeance for the death and displacement of most of his friends and family. That was why he made the long trip to America.

Qasim sat behind Saif and was staring out at the dark landscape. He longed to be back in Syria. Not the Syria he left but the Syria of his childhood. So many things had changed in the last few years since the civil war began. He too blamed the Americans for not stopping the Syrian government from oppressing his people. Qasim had traveled with his brother to Mexico before, coming into the United States with Saif. Qasim's brother had been apprehended by the Mexican police the night before they were to enter the

United States. Qasim vowed to go back to Laredo and retrieve his brother if he survived this job.

Jackson sat behind Nigel. Like Nigel, he had grown up in Detroit; and like many black men in his neighborhood, he had grown restless and disgruntled toward the United States government. Much of his angst was toward the current president, who had promised a better life for many but had delivered nothing. Everyone whom he knew was worse off than when this president entered office. Jackson had met the rest of the team at the compound located just south of Detroit. He didn't share their religion. He didn't have any religion. He didn't believe that any god could exist and allow so many horrible things to happen to his people, but Jackson shared his anger for the United States government that the other three men shared. That was their bond. These four men had trained together for only a few weeks and really didn't know one another very well, but they knew one another well enough to pull off the job.

CHAPTER 7

Christopher

The City of Lights was alive with the sounds of cars and people. The city seemed ready to burst at the seams. The population of Paris had increased by hundreds of thousands as tourists filled every hotel in preparation for the festivities of the coming New Year. The plans for this year's celebration were unprecedented.

Christopher had been stationed here since Thanksgiving. His apartment was at a walking distance to the Louvre, and he could see the Eiffel Tower a short distance away. Langley placed him in France to sniff out ISIS cells who presumably were planning to attack France soon. He had a support staff of two, and that really ticked him off. If the CIA really thought that something big was going to happen in Paris, then why didn't they give him more people? He could barely follow one cell with the resources at his disposal.

In the past twelve months, global tensions increased as ISIS, also known as the Islamic State, continued to increase its presence around the world. Refugees had flooded into many European countries from war-torn Syria. They had come from Syria and into France at an alarming rate, and they were disappearing at an even more alarming rate. Christopher had warned the CIA headquarters at Langley multiple times that he needed more resources to track all the potential hostiles. But so far, no additional support had arrived. According to his supervisor, he probably wouldn't receive any help until the coming spring.

Christopher was looking out over the city, wondering what he had done to deserve this assignment, when one of his support team called in.

"Hey, Chris, I'm on my way in. Can I get you anything?" the soft voice said.

Sara had been with the CIA for just over a year. She graduated second in her class and was an expert marksman, as well as a pretty good linguist. Sara had been assigned to Chris just three months ago, primarily because she spoke fluent French as well as Arabic. She had long dark hair and blue eyes, and she was becoming a distraction for Chris.

"Thanks, Sara!" Chris answered. "How about a coffee from that place down the street?"

"Okay, how about a sandwich or something?" Sara asked.

"Umm, yeah sure. That sounds good," Chris replied. "Surprise me!"

When Chris first met Sara, he thought she was beautiful. Too beautiful in fact for a CIA agent. He had heard that she came from money and simply wanted to serve her country. Chris liked that about her. He played the role of boss for the first two months that they worked together, but she softened him up over the last several weeks.

She hadn't been flirting with him or anything; she just had a great personality and was really easy to get along with. Chris and Sara shared many of the same interests, and under different circumstances, Chris thought that he could become close to her, even though she was almost fifteen years younger than him. The other problem was that Chris didn't think that Sara had romantic feelings for him.

"Hey, old man!" Ed said as he came into the apartment.

Ed had been with the agency for almost seven years. He was an arrogant womanizer, and he was constantly hitting on Sara, which really made Chris mad. But Sara made an art of rejecting Ed, so Chris never said anything. Chris thought that Ed probably realized that Sara was out of his league and was now just playing a game.

"Any news from downtown?" Chris asked Ed. He had asked Ed to contact the French police to get any updates that might help with their surveillance.

"No!" Ed exclaimed. "Those French jerks have their heads stuck so far up their own..." he trailed off.

"I don't understand why they aren't more helpful," Chris stated. "We are only trying to help keep their people safe."

"Yeah, I know. I don't get it either," Ed said as he sat down, shaking his head.

"Hey, where's little Miss America?" Ed asked with a smile.

Chris looked over at him with a frown and simply shook his head.

"Okay, okay, where is sweet little Miss Sara?" Ed asked with a bigger smile.

Chris continued to shake his head but relented. "She's on her way up," Chris said with a smile. "She's grabbing me a sandwich and coffee."

"Dude, she totally has a thing for you. When are you going to take a run at her?" Ed asked. He always had a way of saying the simplest things in the crudest way possible.

"I am not going to—" Chris started to say as the door of the apartment opened. Sara had her hands full with coffee and sandwiches. She slightly turned and kicked the door closed. Chris found delight in her simple movements.

Inside his mind, Chris was thinking, *Dude, you really have to focus and stop with this nonsense. She'd never want to go out with an old man like you.* He was hardly old, but turning forty last year had really made him feel old. He didn't get the music that was popular these days, and he certainly didn't understand the current fashion trends, especially those worn by young Parisians.

"What?" Sara exclaimed.

Dang it! Chris thought to himself. He must have been staring at her again. "Sorry," he said out loud. "I just have a lot on my mind." He turned away from Sara and back toward the window.

Sara smiled and continued, "Well, I have a ham-and-turkey sandwich for both of you old men."

Chris cringed a bit and then turned back to Sara. Before he could say anything, Ed cleared his throat and blurted out, "I'm hardly old, little Miss Sunshine. You must be talking to grandpa over there." Ed motioned to Chris.

Chris glared at him and took the sandwich from Sara with a smile. "Thanks, Sara," Chris said. She smiled and sat down next to him.

They ate their food and drank their coffee in silence for a few minutes before Chris would brief them on the day's assignments.

CHAPTER 8

Ford

The snow was gently falling outside as Ford sipped his coffee. He had just finished his breakfast and was thinking about the connections between the book of Daniel and the book of Revelation. In front of him were all the notes that he had gathered over the years. Months prior, he had come to realize that all the prophetic passages in the book of Daniel were pointing to the same event. Those passages were giving us a road map to the events that would occur prior to the second coming of Jesus.

Ford turned to the section on Daniel 2 and began to read. In Daniel chapter 2, the prophet describes a dream that Nebuchadnezzar, the king of Babylon at the time, had of a multilayered statue. The statue had a head of gold, the chest and arms of silver, the belly and thighs of bronze, the legs of iron, and the feet and toes of iron and clay. The prophet Daniel explained to Nebuchadnezzar what each layer of the statue meant. He went on to say that the head of gold was the kingdom of Babylon. The chest and arms of silver represented a kingdom that would follow Babylon, but this kingdom would be inferior. The belly and thighs of bronze represented yet another kingdom, but one that would rule the entire earth. The legs of iron represented a kingdom that was as strong as iron, and it would break and smash everything.

The feet and toes of mixed iron and clay would represent a kingdom that was partially strong and partially brittle. It would be a divided kingdom that would not remain united. Daniel went on to say that in those days, God would set up a kingdom that would never be destroyed, nor would it be left to another people. It would crush all those kingdoms and bring them to an end, but it would itself endure forever. This last kingdom would be the kingdom ruled by Jesus after his second coming.

At the time of Daniel, the identity of these future kingdoms—represented by silver, bronze, iron, and iron and clay—was unknown. Ford knew that their identities could be discovered through research and study, by tying all the prophecy from the book of Daniel together and by observing the historical record.

Ford paused to let that information sink in. His coffee was still warm but was running low. He decided to get up and walk into the kitchen so that he could top off his cup. As he poured, he continued to contemplate everything that he just read. Up until recent years, most commentators had not connected the dots between the various dreams and visions that Daniel had. Recently, a few authors had begun to draw those lines.

With his fresh cup of coffee, Ford sat down and continued to review his notes. In Daniel chapter 7, the prophet had a dream of four beasts that came up out of the sea. The first beast was that of a lion with wings of an eagle. Its wings were torn off, and it was lifted up from the ground so that it stood like a man. It was given the heart of a man. The second beast looked like a bear that was raised up on one side. It had three ribs in its mouth, and it was told to "get up and eat your fill of flesh." The third beast looked like a leopard. It had four wings like those of a bird. It had four heads and was given authority to rule. The fourth beast was a terrifying and frightening beast. It had large iron teeth. It crushed and devoured its victims and trampled underfoot what was left. This beast was different and had ten horns.

While Daniel was thinking about the ten horns, a little horn came up among them. It uprooted three of the original ten horns. This little horn had the eyes of a man and a mouth that spoke boastfully. The dream continued with God slaying the fourth beast and throwing it into the blazing fire. Daniel was troubled by this dream and was given an interpretation. The four beasts represented four kingdoms that would rise from the earth. The fourth beast, the terrifying and frightening beast, was the fourth kingdom that would rise up. It would devour the whole earth. Out of it would come ten kingdoms represented by the ten horns. After them, another king, represented by the little horn, would rise and subdue the three kings, represented by the three horns that were uprooted. This king represented the Antichrist. He would speak against God and would try to change the set times and the laws. "The saints will be handed over to him for a time, times, and half a time" (Daniel 7:25).

Ford continued to stare out the windows on the cold December afternoon. Snow had been falling for days, and it was clear that winter had taken its hold. Only time would change that. He looked down at his empty cup of coffee and contemplated filling it again. He knew that he should probably hold off because if he had another cup, he'd probably be bouncing off the walls.

Rather than take a break, Ford decided to continue to organize his thoughts. He listed the kingdoms in his head as if to reinforce everything that he'd learned over the past several years of study. Historically, he knew that the kingdom that followed the Babylon Empire was the Medo-Persian Empire; after that, the Greek Empire. It was the fourth kingdom represented by the legs of iron in Daniel 2 and by the terrifying beast in Daniel 7 that had caused so much controversy over the years. For the longest time, most people believed that this kingdom was that of the Roman Empire; but as the book of Daniel was unsealed and became clearer, that conclusion became less likely.

Ford used the word *unsealed* in conversation with others many times, and he always had to explain what he meant. It could be frustrating when something so obvious to him was so unclear to others, but only years of study had made things this clear to him.

Daniel 12:8–9 reads, "I heard, but I did not understand. So I asked, 'My Lord, what will the outcome of all this be?' He replied, 'Go your way, Daniel, because the words are closed up and sealed until the time of the end.'"

Daniel was told that this prophecy would not be fully understood until the time of the end. Ford laughed because this was more proof that the time of the end was upon us. More and more information about Daniel's prophecy had been made clear over the last decade. The book of Daniel was being unsealed so that those who were watchers could share with everyone what was about to happen.

Ford shook his head and returned to his notes. Historically, many have believed that the Antichrist would emerge out of the revived Roman Empire. The problem with this theory was that when you examine both the "legs of iron" from Daniel 2 and the "terrifying beast" from Daniel 7, you realize that both of these scriptures don't point to the Roman Empire. The Roman Empire didn't crush when it conquered;

it assimilated other cultures into its own. For example, when the Roman Empire conquered the Greek Empire, it took the Greek gods, changed their names, and made them their own. This is only one example. What history shows is that there was another empire out there that exemplified both the "legs of iron" and the "terrifying beast." That empire is the Islamic caliphate, and it crushed and destroyed the people, religions, and cultures of all the nations that it conquered.

At its height, the Islamic caliphate conquered the entire Middle East, all of North Africa, parts of Asia, and parts of Europe. By the 1500s, it had become known as the Ottoman Empire, and it ruled up until the end of World War I. The Ottomans joined forces with Germany and Austria as part of the Axis armies of World War I. After being defeated by the Allied forces, the Ottoman Empire was broken up and divided into what now is the modern nations of the Middle East. At that time, the caliphate was abolished for the first time since its creation in the AD seventh century. Only recently has the caliphate been reestablished by the Islamic State, also known as ISIS.

So many thoughts were running through Ford's head. The "terrifying beast" of Daniel 7 was reminiscent of another beast. Ford flipped through his notes and found the section on the book of Revelation, specifically chapter 17. The book of Revelation, chapter 17, discussed another beast, this one with seven heads. It was explained that these heads represented kingdoms. It was said that "five of the kingdoms have fallen"—"one is" and "one who has not yet come." It was said that the seventh kingdom would remain for a time. At the time the book of Revelation was written, the Roman Empire ruled most of the known world. The Roman Empire was identified as the "one [that] is." The previous five kingdoms were Egypt, Assyria, Babylon, Persia, and Greece. History also tells us that each of these kingdoms or empires persecuted the Jews. The Romans, to some degree, also persecuted the Jews. The biggest question that remained was what kingdom was the "one who has not yet come"? The kingdom that conquered the Roman Empire was the Islamic caliphate. So the Islamic caliphate was also the only empire that exemplified the "iron legs" and the "terrifying beast." This scripture also said that the seventh kingdom would remain awhile, and after it was gone, an eighth kingdom would arrive, and it would come out of the seventh.

Ford found it incredible that the Islamic caliphate also matched the seventh kingdom found in Revelation 17. It was the kingdom that came after the Roman Empire, and it remained awhile. The Islamic caliphate reemerged only recently, and it was possible that the new Islamic caliphate was the beginning of what would become the eighth beast empire.

Ford stood up from his desk and walked to the window. The snow had quit falling, and the sun was starting to show through the weakening clouds. If he had stood there much longer, he would have had to either put on some sunglasses or would have become snow-blind. He smiled to himself and decided that he would continue his review for a few more minutes before heading out to the barn to work on a few projects.

Ford picked up a new stack of paper regarding some recent research that he had been working on. Lately, more and more of his time was spent on the book of Revelation. The section he wanted to focus on was chapter 13. The book of Revelation chapter 13 talked about a beast out of the sea with ten horns and seven heads. This beast was given its power by Satan. This beast represented the Antichrist and the empire that he would control. It was also said that one of its heads seemed to have a fatal wound but that the fatal wound had been healed, and the whole world was astonished and followed the beast.

Ford reread his notes and found it increasingly astonishing that all these scriptures pointed to the same thing. The beast in Revelation 13 was more proof that the Revived Islamic caliphate was the eighth beast army that would be ruled by the Antichrist. The Revived Islamic caliphate was also the "feet of iron and clay" found in Daniel 2. It was also the "little horn" found in Daniel 7. All these scriptures continued to point to the same thing.

It was clear to Ford that the Islamic caliphate was the "legs of iron" from Daniel 2, as well as the "terrifying beast" from Daniel 7. It also became clear to Ford that the Greek Empire was the "belly and thighs of bronze" in Daniel 2 and the "beast that resembled a leopard" in Daniel 7. Additionally, he realized that the "chest and arms of silver" in Daniel 2 and the "beast that resembled a bear" in Daniel 7 pointed to the Medo-Persian Empire. Lastly, Ford identified the "head of gold" in Daniel 7 and the "beast that resembled a lion" in Daniel 7 as the Babylonian Empire.

Ford smiled and nodded. "So 'the feet of iron and clay' from Daniel 2 and the 'little horn' from Daniel 7 both point to the Antichrist and the empire that he would rule!" Ford said aloud. "So much has been made clear over the last year or so, but more has to be figured out. There are several other chapters in Daniel and Ezekiel that need to be tied in." He paused. "There are parts of Isaiah and other books as well, not to mention the rest of Revelation," he continued to mumble to himself.

After a pause, he asked himself, "Has the first seal truly been opened? And are we about to witness the opening of the second   seal?"

CHAPTER 9

Samantha

A couple of weeks had passed since Sam witnessed the strange weather phenomenon outside her home near Bernalillo, New Mexico. The Sandia Mountains now had snow on their peaks, and Sam was sure that the mountains were packed with skiers and other outdoor adventurers. Rob had suggested just last night that they take the weekend and head up to his parents' cabin in the mountains. This time of year, it could be difficult to get there because of the snow, but Rob's father said that, for now, the roads were clear. The great thing about this retreat was that it was surrounded by nature, and you couldn't help but feel closer to God way up in the mountains. Normally, Sam would have the boys stay with friends, but she still felt like something big was about to happen. She knew that Rob wanted a weekend without kids so that they could reconnect.

Just like every marriage, she and Rob had their ups and downs. God had blessed them with mostly good times, and Sam was eternally thankful. Right now their marriage was as good as ever, but they did need some alone time together. Work and family can sometimes get in the way if it is allowed. Last night Sam had asked if they could bring the boys, but Rob insisted that they go alone. Normally, Rob would concede to whatever Sam wanted, but this time, she could tell that he really needed them to be alone. Sam had relented, but it didn't make her stop worrying. The reality was that neither Jacob nor Isaac would really want to be up at the cabin anyway.

Jacob had just turned eighteen and was in his senior year of high school. He would rather spend time with friends than hang out with his family. This was pretty typical of most teenagers. Sam knew that he loved his family, but he also wanted his freedom. On more than one occasion, he had commented on how he couldn't wait to go to college. He had decided that he would attend the University of New Mexico in Albuquerque. He was so excited to leave home, yet he didn't want to go too far away. She loved him for that. Just a few years ago, Jacob would have jumped at the chance to go to the cabin. He loved being out in the forest, surrounded by nature. He loved to hike and ride mountain bikes. He had been a boy scout since the age of ten and was becoming quite the survivalist. They didn't have any guns in their home, but Jacob's friend Ramon was an avid hunter. Ramon and his father had taken Jacob hunting a few times. It turned out that Jacob was an excellent marksman with both firearms and bows.

Now Isaac, on the other hand, loved being at home. He was very loving to both Sam and Rob. He was a sophomore in high school and was an excellent musician. He excelled at multiple instruments, including percussion, piano, and guitar. He also excelled in academics and currently was a straight A student. Isaac had a great ear for music and loved all varieties. He could listen to a song, and within a short time, he would be playing it fairly well. He never ceased to amaze Sam. However, even though Isaac loved being with his family, he wasn't a big fan of the cabin. Sam would have to figure out where to send him.

"Hey, Isaac," Sam started, "You know Dad and I are going up to the cabin for the weekend, right?"

"Yeah," Isaac replied. He was eating his cereal before getting ready for school.

"Well, where would you like to stay?" Sam asked.

"Can't I stay home with Jacob?" Isaac replied.

"Honey, I don't think that is a good idea," Sam began. "Jacob is fine by himself, but I'm not sure I like the idea of just the two of you here alone."

"Okay, how about Jack's house?" Isaac asked.

Sam knew Jack's parents a little, and they seemed to be nice people. But as far as she knew, they didn't go to church very often. She would have preferred that Isaac stay with a strong Christian family, especially with everything that was going on in the world.

"Okay, let me call Jack's mom and find out," Sam started. "If they can't have you, who else would you like to hang out with?" she asked.

"Hmmm, probably Robert or Joel," Isaac answered. Sam was close with Joel's mom, Veronica. They both attended the same Bible study on Wednesdays. Sam knew that Veronica was a Christian. She didn't know about Joel's father, but he seemed like a nice guy.

"Isaac, how about I ask Joel's mother first?" Sam asked. "I really like his mom, and I know the two of you get along pretty good."

"Okay," Isaac replied.

He was always so easygoing. That was another thing that she loved about him. Really, there wasn't anything not to love.

She smiled to herself. "Okay, I'll let you know after school," she said.

Just then, Jacob came out of his bedroom and told Isaac that he was ready to go.

"Aren't you going to get some breakfast, dear?" Sam asked Jacob.

"No time, Mom. I'll get something at school," Jacob replied. "Come on, man, we gotta go!" Jacob added to Isaac.

Isaac lifted his bowl and drank the remaining milk. He got up and put the bowl in the sink. He grabbed his lunch and gave Sam a quick hug.

"Love ya, Mom!" Isaac yelled as he walked out the door.

"Love you too! I love both of you!" Sam exclaimed as she waved them off to school. She looked back at the kitchen table. She shook her head and smiled to herself. "When is he ever going to remember to put the milk and cereal away?" she asked herself out loud.

Sam cleaned up the kitchen and got herself ready to go to work. She would call Veronica during her lunch hour to find out if Isaac could stay there for the weekend. She really hoped that he could because she was really concerned about this coming weekend, especially with Sunday being New Year's Eve.

CHAPTER 10

General Hasim

A year ago, the patrols that moved throughout the compound had been far less numerous than they were today. In the ten years since this underground cavern was completed, the military population had increased to over 250,000. This installation had become the jewel of the Iranian military complex. Construction had begun in secret in the early 1990s, shortly after the succession of the current Ayatollah. It had taken almost ten years to finish the first phase of the underground military base, which originally housed over 150,000 personnel. Over the course of the next several years the capacity was increased to over 350,000, with tunnels extending almost twenty-five miles to the west of Shush, almost reaching the border with Iraq. During the time of the prophet Daniel, this city would have been named Susa.

The original purpose of the military base had been to provide better offensive capability against the Iraqis, if necessary. However, since the Americans had removed Saddam Hussein in the early 2000s, a new purpose was conceived. The Ayatollah desired to rebuild the Persian Empire of old. He had established a presence in Lebanon, Syria, Iraq, Yemen, and other areas throughout the Middle East. He supplied guns and money to terrorist organizations throughout the world. He conceived a plan to destabilize the

United States so that they could not stop him from his conquest of the Middle East. Over the past few years, Iran had held discussions with the Russian leadership, and they were very supportive of the plan from the beginning.

General Hasim, of the Iranian Revolutionary Guard Corps (IRGC), had helped build a comprehensive plan to conquer the Middle East and beyond. The Ayatollah's influence on the American president had also helped by convincing him to leave Iraq under Iranian control. Most of the world didn't realize it, but currently, the Iraqi government was affectively being run by the Ayatollah in Iran. One unexpected outcome of the United States leaving the area was the rise of ISIS. Originally, this development had concerned the general, but over time, he realized that it would be the catalyst for the global acceptance of the Iranian occupation of Iraq.

The Russians had been eager to help Iran because the perceived instability in the region would cause the price of oil to rise. A higher oil price was essential for the continued growth of the Russian economy. With ISIS taking a foothold in Syria and Iraq and with the withdrawal of the United States from the region, it became easier for Russia to back their allies in the current Syrian government. Backing the Syrians would also help Iran, so it was a win-win win.

General Hasim stood in the command center watching the security staff monitor everything from troop movements to weather patterns. In the coming days, the readiness of his army would be tested. Once operation Charging Ram began, Hasim would have tactical control over the majority of Iran's military. This would give him unprecedented power, never before seen in Iran. General Hasim had been a follower of the

Ayatollah for a long time, but he was beginning to wonder if his time had come.

CHAPTER 11

Zack

The wind blew through the fingered hills of Northeastern Wyoming. It seemed to pick up speed as it moved through the valleys. The average temperatures here were normally in the mid-thirties, but this year, they were unseasonably low in the tens, with wind-chill factors of negative ten degrees Fahrenheit or so. Today it was exceptionally cold, and the winds were taking their toll on Zack.

Zack had lived in Wyoming for almost twenty years now, and he had become accustomed to the hard winters. But the last month had been extremely difficult on him. He lived on a forty-acre homestead a few miles north of the famous Devil's Tower from *Close Encounters of the Third Kind* fame. During the summer months, the area was streaming with tourists and other undesirables, so Zack stayed away from the place, for the most part. More often, he would hike through the miles of trails during the colder fall months and occasionally in the winter.

Zack's homestead was almost completely off the grid. He had installed solar panels on the house and barn and had also installed a pair of wind generators. He had virtually all the power he needed. In addition to being mostly off the grid, Zack had a desire to be completely self-sufficient. He had a large garden and a big flock of chickens that provided both meat and eggs. He was also an avid hunter, so he was rarely short on a supply of meat.

As tensions with the current government increased, Zack had become increasingly paranoid. Because of this, he had installed a complete underground shelter that was stocked with enough food and water to last him several years. He had more guns and ammo than a small army. But unfortunately, he had no one to share it with.

Today he was tracking a deer that he had shot about an hour ago. A stray branch had deflected Zack's arrow slightly off its mark, which resulted in less-than-a-clean kill. The deer would die, but its adrenaline had propelled its flight by more than a mile. The bed of snow helped to track his prey, and he could tell by the tracks and the blood trail that he would soon meet his prize. The problem was getting her back to his camp. Normally Zack would have harvested a buck, but his meat freezer was getting low, so he decided to take a mature doe.

"Come on, baby, where are you?" Zack whispered. Over the years, he had become accustomed to talking to himself in a whisper. On occasion, he caught himself doing it and would laugh, but he didn't really care. Living a solitary life tends to make you a little crazy at times.

Zack rounded the trail, and there she was. She had made quite an effort to get away, but fate wasn't on her side. Zack knelt down next to her and pressed his hand against her neck. She felt warm to his touch, and her fur had a familiar feel to it.

"Thanks, sweetheart," he said. He had always acknowledged the harvest and was thankful every time. He wasn't really spiritual, but he felt a oneness with the world when he harvested an animal. He was pretty sure there was a God out there, but Zack didn't have much contact with Him. But during moments like this, he wondered. There was something spiritual about the process of harvesting a deer.

It only took him a few minutes to field dress the deer. He knew that the deer's organs wouldn't go to waste. Within the hour, some creature would make its way toward the pile, and the circle of life would continue. He was glad that he had brought the sled along because pulling her out without it would be next to impossible these days. In his twenties, dragging a deer like this a mile or two wouldn't be too bad, but now in his mid-forties, it was getting more difficult. The sled would make it a lot easier. He would be tired by the time he got home, but he would make it.

The trip home didn't take him nearly as long as he thought it would. He was a little tired, but not too bad. He hung the deer up in the barn and closed the door for the night. He would finish processing her in the morning. For now, he was simply satisfied to get cleaned up and go make some dinner.

During the winter months, Zack would most often take his dinner in front of the fireplace. He enjoyed watching the flames dance and tumble. He could sit there for hours, but tonight, he had other things to do. It had been a while since he had contacted his old high school buddy, and with the New Year coming up, he thought that now would be a good time to check in. He strode up to his desk and opened the laptop. This machine was out of place in the cabin, but it had its value. Zack only used it a couple of times a month, mostly to catch up on the news and to occasionally e-mail his friends. He laughed at the thought of e-mail. You had to work pretty hard to escape technology these days. Even in the backwoods of Wyoming, the Internet was alive and kicking.

With a smile, Zack sat down and began typing on the keys.

CHAPTER 12

Nigel

The big show was only thirty-six hours away, and Nigel and his team were doing their final preparations. They had been working in the large auditorium for the last couple of hours. Their assignment was to prepare the final cable connections to the in-house audio system. In addition to that, they had delivered their real payload that consisted of a cylinder the size of a beer keg. This cylinder looked and functioned like an electronic transformer. This transformer was responsible for distributing power to all aspects of the video and sound system.

As Nigel finalized the connections, he recalled the conversation that he had with Ali many weeks ago back at the compound when Nigel and his team had just successfully finished their dry run of connecting the transformer.

"Nigel, your team is ready, and God willing, you will prevail," Ali had said as he patted Nigel on the back.

Nigel had felt a swell in his heart as Ali filled a void in Nigel's life. Nigel had never known his father, and finally, he had a man in his life who could fill that role.

Nigel had bowed his head and thanked Ali. "Thank you, Ali. We could not have done it without your training and support."

"Allahu Akbar!" Ali had said.

"Allahu Akbar!" Nigel had repeated with a smile.

Back in the auditorium, Nigel opened the transformer and set the timer for 11:00 p.m. for the following night. He peeked inside one last time and admired the eloquent device that would strike terror in the hearts of every American. The thick blue liquid shimmered in the light. It was virtually undetectable by conventional bomb-sniffing dogs and electronic equipment. The liquid was very similar to the napalm that was used during the Vietnam War. When an electronic charge was applied to the liquid, it would quickly expand and fill the room with a highly flammable foamy substance. It was the second charge that would ignite the foam, leading to an explosion that would completely destroy a four-block radius.

Nigel had witnessed a small-scale demo of this explosive, and it was frightening. He had been assured that without an electrical charge, the liquid was completely benign, but it was still a little unnerving being so close to a quantity this size of the blue liquid.

Nigel closed the transformer and waved to Jackson. Jackson nodded and began cleaning up his tools. The detonator was set, and their work was done. The team would go back to the hotel and monitor the area to ensure that their device was not detected. Their backup plan was to come in with guns blazing if the device was found.

Nigel closed his toolbox and watched the rest of the team vacate the room. "Allahu Akbar," he whispered to himself as he walked out.

Many people would die very soon, and America would never be the same after they succeeded in their task. Nigel knew that there were at least three more attacks planned at the same time, but he didn't know where. He suspected that there were more, but only time would tell if he was correct.

CHAPTER 13

Samantha

Everything was all set for the weekend. She had one last thing to do before they left, and that was to call her brother, Brian. They had planned to spend Friday and Saturday at the cabin. Samantha and Rob would celebrate New Year's Eve alone for the first time since they got married.

Sam was really starting to look forward to a few nights alone with her husband. It would be really great to reconnect without the normal distractions that life brought. She had swept her uneasiness about the current state of the world under the proverbial carpet and was ready to relax.

As she completed her mental checklist, she picked up the phone and dialed Brian.

"Umm, hello?" Brian answered with apprehension.

"Hey, Brian, this is Sam," Sam started. "How are you doing?"

"Hey, Sam, I'm doing okay," Brian replied.

It had been a while since she had spoken to Brian, and there seemed to be a little awkward silence between them.

"Mom's says that you have a new girlfriend," Sam inquired.

"Well, she's hardly new. We've been going out for over six months," Brian replied.

"Well, she's new to me," Sam teased. "So what's her name?"

"Her name is Michele," Brian answered.

Sam could tell this conversation would be like pulling teeth at the dentist office. "So where did you meet her?" Sam questioned. She could hear Brian sigh on the other end of the phone.

"I met her at the gym actually," Brian replied.

Again, there was more silence on the line. Sam wondered if they would ever have a normal conversation again. *Like pulling teeth*, Sam thought. "That's nice. So how are you doing, Brian?" Sam asked.

"I'm fine," he replied.

Sam was getting frustrated at Brian's short answers, but she could hardly blame anyone but herself for not talking to him for so long. Sam couldn't believe it, but it must have been at least nine months since she had spoken to him.

"Brian, I'm so sorry that I haven't called you in a while," Sam apologized. "I'm not a very good big sister."

"It's okay. I haven't called you either," Brian replied and seemed to soften a bit after her apology.

Sam wondered if maybe he had been upset that she hadn't talked to him in a while.

"I do wish you lived closer though," Brian said.

"Yeah, me too," Sam replied. Since she was ten years older than Brian, she had often been given the responsibility of babysitting him when he was young. She remembered spending time reading to him and playing various learning games. Her mother had insisted that they not watch television and only play educational games.

"How are Rob and the boys?" Brian asked.

Sam could almost feel him opening up further. "They are doing well," Sam replied.

"When are you coming home again?" Brian asked.

"I'm going to try to get there this summer," Sam replied.

"Oh, that would be awesome!" Brian exclaimed, and he almost seemed excited about it.

"So how's everything else going, Brian?" Sam asked.

"Life is good for the most part. Michele and I are pretty happy. I wasn't sure about her having a kid, but he's not too bad," Brian replied.

Sam chuckled a little. "How old is he?" Sam asked.

"He is two," Brian said. "Michele got married a year after graduating from college. They got pregnant a couple of days before her husband got deployed to Iraq. He died there."

Sam was happy that Brian was opening up.

"When I met Michele, she was up front about her child and dead husband. For the first time in my life, I wasn't afraid about children. Sam, there is something special about Michele," Brian said. "She said that her husband's death had been very difficult, and she told me that the only thing that had gotten her through was her belief in God," he added. Brian paused a little, and Sam sensed that he wanted to say more, so she waited.

"I wasn't so sure about any of the God stuff. I guess I believe there is a God, but I don't know," Brian shared.

"What aren't you sure about?" Sam asked.

"Well, I don't get this whole Jesus thing. I never really paid attention in church, I guess. I don't see how believing in Jesus makes a difference," Brian said. "Why does any of it matter?" he asked.

Sam wasn't going to miss out on an opportunity to talk about Jesus, and she jumped right in. "Well, as a Christian, we believe that Jesus is the Son of God and that he was born of the Virgin Mary. We believe that he was crucified and died on the cross. The cool part is that he rose from the dead three days later," Sam said.

"But why does that matter?" Brian interrupted.

"Well, before Jesus, the only way to be cleansed of sin was through a sacrifice on the altar, specifically at the temple in Jerusalem," Sam replied.

"But, I thought that was a Jewish thing?" Brian questioned.

"It was a Jewish thing, I guess, because at the time, only the Jews worshiped our God. All others were worshiping other gods. When Jesus died and rose from the dead, he made a single sacrifice to replace all other sacrifices. All we have to do to be saved is recognize Jesus as our Savior and to accept the sacrifice that He made for us," Sam replied.

"Hmmm. That is interesting," Brian said.

Sam's heart began to fill with the spirit and love for her brother. "Brian, I can show you how to accept Jesus if you want," Sam said. There was a long pause on the phone. "I'm not going to pressure you. I just want you to be happy and to be saved," she added.

"Thanks, sis. I will think about it," he replied.

Sam's heart sank a bit, but she was glad to have had a chance to talk to him about Jesus, even if it was so brief.

"Sam, I should get going," Brian said. "Thanks for calling me. I miss you."

"I miss you too, Brian!" Sam said. "Please call me if you have any questions or if you just want to pray together."

"See ya, Sam," Brian said.

"See ya, Brian," Sam replied.

She hung up the phone and wished that she could have talked more, but she felt like she had made some serious headway toward helping Brian become a Christian. Sam felt the clouds gathering again. She looked outside, but everything was fine. However, deep down, she knew that something big was about to happen.

CHAPTER 14

Christopher

With less than twenty-four hours before the New Year's Eve celebration in Paris, things were getting a little tense among the group. Ed was his normal, erratic self, but it was the change in Sara's mood that concerned Chris the most. Over the past few days, her mood had become as dark as her hair. From outward appearances, Sara seemed like her normal, happy self, but she was hiding something.

It was 6:00 a.m. (Paris time) on December 31, and Ed had just left to go catch a short nap. He had been up for most of the past twenty-four hours, combing through all the intelligence that had begun to flood in. Something big was about to happen, but the team just couldn't connect all the dots. Chris had called the night before for more resources and was denied again. It seemed to him that his superiors almost wanted something to happen. He shook his head and mumbled. *Gotta quit thinking like that!* he thought.

Chris was leafing through the latest social media report when he felt a light touch on his shoulder. More and more, ISIS and other terrorist organizations were using social media, like Twitter and Facebook, to communicate with their fellow jihadist.

Chris turned to see Sara's smiling face. Gosh, she is beautiful! he immediately thought. He shook his head and did his best to smile back. "Hey, what's up?" Chris asked.

With her hand still on his shoulder, she took the seat next to him. Her touch seemed to last forever, and it was all he could bear before she finally moved her hand.

"I was just going over the report from the locals, and there is something that just doesn't jive," Sara replied.

Chris didn't say anything. He just continued to stare at her beautiful blue eyes. After a moment, she looked down at the stack of papers on her lap. She turned the papers to Chris and moved in a little closer to show him what she had found. For the slightest moment, her knee brushed his, and he felt an electric charge move through his body. His face must have reddened because she began to look at him questioningly.

He looked down and began looking at the report as it sat on her lap. Then he moved slowly to pick it up as he realized what it was that had disturbed her. Within the last twelve hours, the amount of chatter had increased by more than ten times. That seemed impossible because the chatter had been ever increasing over the past week or so. At this point, the amount of chatter could only mean that an attack was imminent. Yet the other part of this report seemed to contradict this data as the French authorities had not yet raised the terror level. Based on this data, the terror level should have been set to "imminent" or, at a minimum, "very high"; but right now, it was still only set to "medium." Was there some miscommunication within their government?

"Am I reading this right?" Chris asked. "All indications point to an imminent attack, but their terror level is still only 'medium'?"

"Yes—"

"Did you talk to the police chief?" Chris interrupted.

"Yes, I was just about to say that I talked with Claude less than thirty minutes ago, and he said that the president didn't want to raise the threat level without credible information," Sara explained.

"But just the pure amount of chatter should be enough to raise it to at least 'high'!" Chris exclaimed, raising his voice.

"I agree, Chris, and I think Claude did too," she said. "Although he wouldn't say as much," she added.

"Hmmm, I don't like this at all," Chris said as he looked at the pages and shook his head. "All indications are that something big is coming." He added, "Something real big."

CHAPTER 15

Ford

Abby was sitting in front of the fireplace reading a book. She normally wore her hair in a ponytail, but that night, her shoulder-length dark-blonde hair lay on her shoulders. She wore a thick sweater and had a blanket draped over her legs. Next to her, on the end table, was a steaming cup of hot chocolate. Ford sat down on his chair and stared into the fire. He watched the flames dance and pop in the night. For some reason, neither of them had been able to sleep, so Abby suggested that they build a fire and enjoy the quiet evening together. It was shortly past midnight, and the following night at this time, they would be celebrating the New Year.

Outside, there was a partial moon, and it illuminated the snow-covered yard. All forecasts had predicted a mild winter, but every one of them had been wrong, at least with regard to the amount of snow there would be. So far, there was almost twenty-four inches of snow. Thankfully, it had fallen gradually over the past four weeks and had been manageable for the most part.

Inevitably, Ford's mind wandered to the book of Daniel. More and more, he thought about the words written by the prophet Daniel more than two thousand years ago and how they seemed to be on the verge of fulfillment. Every day, more and more prophecy seemed to come alive with the events of the world.

Ford's most recent studies had provided even more clues to the coming events. In Daniel 8, the prophet had a vision where he found himself in the citadel of Susa, which is located in the southwest region of modern-day Iran. In his vision, he saw a ram with two horns standing beside the canal. The ram charged toward the west, the north, and the south. No animal could stand against him, and none could be rescued from his power. He did as he pleased and became great. The archangel Gabriel was there to interpret the vision for him, and he told Daniel that the ram represented the kings of Media and Persia. History tells us that the Medo-Persian Empire eventually conquered the Babylonian Empire, which was in dominant power during Daniel's lifetime.

Ford recalled a scripture that indicated that Daniel's dreams were represented by historical events that occurred after the days of Daniel but also that they represented future events that would occur in the time of the end.

"Does this mean that Iran will soon make its move to conquer the Middle East?" Ford wondered aloud.

Ford continued reviewing his notes on Daniel 8. Daniel's dream continued by showing a goat with a prominent horn between his eyes coming from the west. The goat charged at the ram in great rage, and he furiously shattered the ram's two horns. The ram was powerless to stand against the goat, and the goat knocked him to the ground and trampled him. None could rescue the ram from the goat's power. The goat then became great, but at the height of his power, his large horn was broken off, and in its place, four prominent horns grew up toward the four winds of heaven. Gabriel continued to interpret the vision and told Daniel that the goat represented the kingdom of Greece and that the original horn represented the first king. The four horns that came later represented four kingdoms that would emerge from his nation but would not have the same power.

Again, Ford was intrigued by the idea that Greece may have some future role in preparing the way for the Antichrist. The only problem was that it did not really make sense given the current state of Greece. Ford picked up another book that was relevant to this scripture. At the height of the Greek Empire, the capital was located in Constantinople, which is modern-day Istanbul, Turkey. More and more commentators agreed that the goat represented Turkey, and Ford tended to agree with them.

Ford continued reading his notes on Daniel 8. Daniel's dream continued with another small horn coming out of one of the four horns. It started small but grew in power to the south and the east and toward the *Beautiful Land*. This horn grew until it almost reached the heavens, and then it threw some of the starry hosts down to the earth and trampled on them. It set itself up to be as great as the Prince of the hosts, and it removed the daily sacrifices. The place of sanctuary would be brought low. The archangel Gabriel interpreted this part of the vision for Daniel as well. He told Daniel that the small horn represented a stern-faced king, a master of intrigue. This king is the Antichrist. He would become very strong, but not by his own power. He would cause astounding devastation and would succeed in whatever he did. He would destroy the mighty men and the holy people. He would cause deceit to prosper, and he would consider himself superior. When the people of Israel felt secure, he would destroy many and take his stand against the Prince of princes, Jesus. Yet the

Antichrist would be destroyed, but not by human power, but by Jesus.

Ford contemplated all of this but then remembered one very interesting verse, Daniel 8:14, which said, "He said to me, 'It will take 2,300 evenings and mornings; then the sanctuary will be reconsecrated.'" This was an answer to the question, How long will it take for the vision to be fulfilled—the vision concerning the daily sacrifices, the rebellion that causes desolation, and the surrender of the sanctuary and of the host that will be trampled underfoot? It is explained that this prophecy concerns the distant future and that it must be sealed up. Again, Daniel was told to seal up the vision so that in the distant future, the time of the end, the prophecy may become clearer.

Ford asked himself, "What is this 2,300 days?" The Bible said that this part of the vision was to be sealed up. "How long until we have an understanding of the 2,300 days?" During Daniel's lifetime, there were 360 days in the calendar. The math says that 2,300 days is 6.39 years, or six years, four months, and twenty days.

"These numbers don't make any sense to me—6.39 years!" he exclaimed in a whisper.

Ford began to realize that Daniel 2, Daniel 7, and Daniel 8 all concerned the same time of the end. Gabriel made it clear that the ram represented Persia. So the ram in Daniel 8 was the same as the "chest and arms of silver" found in Daniel 2 and the same as the "beast that resembles a bear" in Daniel 7. Gabriel also identified Greece as the goat with one horn. So the goat with one horn in Daniel 8 was the same as the "belly and thighs of bronze" found in Daniel 2 and the same as the "beast that resembles a leopard" found in Daniel 7. Furthermore, the goat with four horns in Daniel 8 would be the same as the "legs of iron" found in Daniel 2 and the same as the "terrifying beast" found in Daniel 7. The small horn in Daniel 8 corresponded to the "feet of iron and clay" found in Daniel 2 and to the "little horn" found in Daniel 7.

To Ford, more and more, the story was becoming clear. The entire book of Daniel seemed to be of the same vision, this vision being a picture of ancient history but also a picture of the future and time of the end. A picture of the Antichrist was becoming clearer. Ford knew that we should be watching for the return of Jesus, but he also knew that the Antichrist would come first. And by watching for him, Ford would know better that Jesus would come soon. Regardless, Ford knew that time would be short, and many more souls needed to be saved.

Ford looked over to Abby, who seemed to have finally fallen asleep. He got up, pulled her blanket up tighter, and decided that he would let her sleep for a little bit. His mind was racing with the story that was forming in his brain.

"What will the future bring?" he asked himself.

Ford had been following the news, especially with regard to Iran. Iran had continued to strengthen its hold on the Middle East. Ford wondered how long until the Persian ram (Iran) charged out to the west (Syria and Iraq), to the north (Turkey), and to the south (Saudi Arabia).

"No one can stop the ram?"Ford mumbled questioningly. "The United States could stop the ram!" he exclaimed to himself.

Ford thought about the current president of the United States, and it seemed to be clear that he was on the side of Iran. The president had enabled Iran at every turn. He had created a deal that gave Iran a path to nuclear weapons. Ford shook his head. He couldn't understand how the Republican controlled Congress would allow him to make such deals. The president had strengthened Iran by removing all the sanctions that had been in place since the 1980s. Ford wondered if our government cared at all about the safety of the American people.

Ford continued his thoughts aloud and said, "But the Bible says that no one *could* stop the ram, not that no one *would* stop the ram." Ford noticed that Abby had moved a bit on her chair, so he decided that he would go into his office and think out loud. He got up, grabbed his Bible, and began walking down the hall.

"Does that mean that something is going to happen that will cause the United States to be powerless?" Ford wondered as he moved away from the family room.

The thought was inconceivable, yet there it was in the Bible. Ford wracked his brain, trying to come up with answers that would make sense. Everything pointed to the realization of end-times events right now. Prophecy seemed to be fulfilled almost daily.

"The Bible is infallible, and because the United States is clearly not found in Bible prophecy, it is very likely that it means that something would soon destabilize the United States to the point that it would lose its status as the lone world power!" Ford exclaimed.

He sat down on his office chair with a thump. "How is this possible?" Ford wondered aloud. "And how much time do we have before it happens?" He stared out the window at the falling snow. Then he heard the familiar sound of e-mail being delivered to his computer.

CHAPTER 16

General Hasim

General Hasim had just received word that the mobilization would most likely begin in two weeks. There were some strategic operations that had to be executed first so that the Americans would not be in a position to act against Iran. His Russian contact would not share the details of the operation but was clear on the timeline. There was a slim part of him that wondered if he should believe the Russians. The Ayatollah had said to trust him, so he was doing his best, but he had never been one to trust an infidel, especially an infidel who said he was on your side.

Iran had freely been running air missions over most of Iraq and in parts of Syria for some time now. In Syria, they had been escorted by Russian Mig-29s. Most of the missions included hitting ISIS targets, but most recently, they had also been softening up the Syrian rebel positions. All these missions were in preparation for the real mission that was to begin in two weeks. They would be mobilizing hundreds of thousands of ground forces. They would be flying hundreds and potentially thousands of bombing raids. The navy would be executing strategic maneuvers as well. The Iranian war machine would also have support from the Russians and the Chinese. The Chinese support would be limited, but according to Russia, it would be vital to the demise of the Americans.

General Hasim's entire military career had led up to this moment. His father probably wouldn't admit it if he was alive, but he would have been proud of his son. Hasim's father never showed any affection. That just wasn't the way of his family. Expectations were set, and expectations were met. It was as simple as that.

General Hasim put out the order that the base's readiness level be set to its highest. This meant that no one was allowed to leave the base for any reason. Under normal circumstances, the penalty for leaving without permission would have been thirty days in the brig. But Hasim had ordered that all defectors be shot on-site. No external communications were allowed to civilian parties, and all military transmissions had to be approved by the general's five commanders. All communications had to be validated so that absolutely no information regarding the pending mission could be leaked.

Soon the world would know of the power that Iran possessed. Even the Russians had been kept in the dark. Twenty stories below the surface of the desert lay the secret that would change the world. General Hasim looked through the observation window as the special projects team finalized their preparation of the weapon. The world knew about the Iranians' missile capability, but they didn't know about this. No one did. But soon Iran would enlighten the Middle East and the rest of the world.

CHAPTER 17

Samantha

The cabin was covered with a few inches of snow. Normally, at this time of the year, there could be a foot or two of snow. Sam and Rob were happy to find the cabin in good working order. Rob went to start up the generator and get the power running while Sam unpacked the Jeep. They had brought their snowshoes just in case there was enough snow. Instead, they probably would settle for a short hike through the woods.

Sam had just gotten their bags in the cabin when the lights came on. She heard the hum of the refrigerator as it came to life. A moment later, Rob came in, holding an armload of wood, and he immediately got to work on building a fire.

"Hey, Rob, when you're done with that, could you bring in the cooler?" Sam asked. "It's a little heavy for me."

"Sure, Babe." Rob replied with a smile.

Sam could tell that Rob was happy to be in the woods. She was happy too. They loved the cabin because it provided just enough of a rustic feel, but they still had electricity and plumbing. There were no televisions or computers. There was a radio that they used on occasion, but mostly for listening to music. One recent improvement was that they had pretty good cell coverage since the new cell tower was put up at the ski resort, which was a few miles away.

The cabin was an older log cabin with two bedrooms and a bathroom. It was just one level, but it had vaulted ceilings between the whole log rafters that spanned the ceiling every two feet. A green steel roof was installed a couple of years ago, so it kind of reminded Sam of one of those old Lincoln Log Homes that she played with as a child.

The inside was decorated as you would expect a log cabin in the mountains to be, but the kitchen had all the modern conveniences of home, including a dishwasher, electric stove, and refrigerator.

As Sam was bringing in the last of the groceries, Rob brought in the cooler.

"Can you set it right there by the refrigerator?"Sam asked.

"Sure, babe," Rob replied. He set it down where she asked and then gave her a light kiss on the cheek.

After checking the fire, Rob went back outside to finish unpacking the Jeep.

Sam was so happy to be at the cabin. Everything seemed perfect, and as she finished unpacking the cooler and groceries, Rob came in from outside.

"Sam, you have to see this!" Rob said. His eyes were lit up with amazement. The cabin was built on the western side of the mountain, so sunsets could be incredible. He grabbed her hand and walked her out to the porch.

When she got outside, she was completely amazed. She saw every color of red, orange, and yellow. There were blue and purple and even some shades of green. The sun painted the clouds, as well as the tips of the trees; and when she turned back to look at the mountains, even they were painted by the sun. Rob was right; she had to see that sunset.

"God is good," she said.

"And one heck of an artist," Rob added with a smile and put his arm around her.

They stood like that until the sun was finished painting the sky. When God's light show was done, they walked into the cabin and began preparing dinner. Sam couldn't believe that the New Year was almost upon them. Tomorrow was the last day of the year, and they would celebrate the New Year, right here, together, as it should be. Sam didn't think she could be any happier.

CHAPTER 18

Ford

Ford was about to go to bed when the computer made that familiar *ding* sound. He contemplated reading his e-mail tomorrow, but something made him sit down at his computer and see what was going on.

It was strange to see a message from Zack. He and Zack had known each other since fifth grade and had been friends for a long time. He remembered the day that Zack's family moved in down the street. Ford and his brother had just shoveled off the driveway so that they could play a little winter basketball. Ford laughed at the thought. Early on in their lives, Ford and his younger brother had lived to play sports.

Ronald was two years younger than Ford, but at the time, they were pretty close in size. Ford was a better athlete back then, but Ron would end up being taller and better at most sports. Ford remembered that day when he and Ron saw Zack walking up the street. He was dressed in a one-piece snowsuit. It almost looked like denim, but of course, it wasn't. He wore a goofy hat and boots that were far too big for his feet.

"Hi, ya'll!" Zack said with a flourish. "My name is Zack!"

"Hey, Zack," Ford replied. "My name is Ford, and this is Ron."

"Can I play with ya'll?" Zack asked. It was clear that Zack wasn't from Michigan. He had a twangy accent from somewhere south, as far as Ford could tell.

"So where'd you move from?" Ron asked.

"Kentucky!" Zack said proudly.

"Cool!" Ron said, even though he didn't really know where Kentucky was.

"Hey, we were about to play a little one-on-one basketball," Ford said. "But maybe we could play a game of horse instead. Do you know how to play?"

"Nah, I've never heard of that game," Zack answered.

"It's easy," Ron said.

"Yeah, we'll teach you," Ford added.

Ford could remember that day as if it had happened yesterday. Since that day, he and Zack had been great friends. It turned out that Zack was in the same grade as Ford. All through middle school and high school, they were inseparable. It wasn't until college that they finally went their separate ways. Ford decided to stay close and go to a university in Michigan, but Zack decided to go out west. They stayed in touch as much as anyone could back then. Without cell phones, free long distance, and e-mail, it was pretty difficult, but they managed to stay fairly close— although, over the last several years, Zack had become more distant. Living on your own in the wilderness of Wyoming tends to make you a little crazy.

Zack had married a girl out of college, and they stayed in Wyoming. A few years after they married, she found out that she had cancer. The cancer had spread to her bones and many organs before they had discovered it. She didn't stand a chance and would die less than a year later. After that, Zack had become a recluse, and communication with him was very slim. Ford had always suspected that it was her death that pushed Zack away from God. Ford opened the e-mail and began to read.

Hey, Ford,

What's up? I just wanted to wish you a Happy New Year and all that crap. Same ole, same ole going on here. What's new with you? Blah, blah, blah.

Hey, the real reason I decided to e-mail you was because things have been a little weird lately. I've been having strange dreams lately, and for some reason, I'm compelled to share them with you.

The first one, I was on the beach. LOL, seriously, when am I going to be on a beach? Anyway, I'm sitting there in a camp chair by a fire pit, and I'm watching the ocean. As I'm sitting there, I notice that the water on the shoreline starts retreating. You know what I'm talking about, right? Like it's being sucked back into the ocean. It just keeps going and going until I can't see it anymore. I just sit there and wonder, and then I wake up. Weird, eh? So yeah, I have had that dream several times over that past few months. It never changes; it's just the same dream over and over again.

The second dream is short and stranger yet. I'm walking through this city of glass, and I'm all alone. There are all sorts of buildings—most are normal shapes, but there are some other strange shapes, like spheres, cylinders, and pyramids. They're weird yet cool. The thing is that every one of them is made of glass. Like see-through glass. You can see everything that is going on inside. Anyway, I'm walking down the street looking at the buildings when large objects start falling from the sky. When I say large, I mean like car sized. They're pretty big. Right away, I realize that when the car-sized object hits the ground, they are going to bring down many of the glass buildings. Just as I'm thinking this, the first object hits a pyramid-shaped building. Glass flies everywhere. More and more buildings are destroyed by these falling objects, and then I wake up. I only had that dream once, but it was pretty darn easy to remember.

Okay, the last dream was the weirdest. It started with me being in the mountains at night, watching the stars. I can see the lights of a large city in the valley below. As I'm watching, there is a tremendous light from behind me. I turn and see the flash of light fade into the night. The suddenness of it all frightens me, and as I turn back to the city lights, they all go out. I'm left completely in the dark. It is almost as if all the stars have gone out too. Then I wake up. I had that dream only once as well.

I know you're into all the weird stuff, so I thought maybe you could figure out what it all means hahaha. Maybe you can help me figure out if I've gone completely crazy.

Anyway, sorry this was so long. Hope to hear from you soon.

See ya bro,

Z

Ford read the letter a second time and then a third time. Zack was never one to have prophetic dreams, but Ford was wondering if more prophecy was coming true. There is a verse in the Bible that says that in the time of the end, men will have visions and prophecy. Ford found it interesting that God chose Zack to be a prophet. Ford couldn't help but laugh at that, and he wondered if maybe there was hope for Zack after all.

Ford figured that the first dream represented a tsunami.

"What does it mean?" Ford wondered aloud. "Is it actually a tsunami warning? Is it an earthquake warning? Does it mean something entirely different?"

Ford thought about the glass-city dream. "That is super strange!" he exclaimed. He could not even begin to understand that dream. He decided that he might have to consult others with regard to that one.

Ford also found the dream about the lights going out strange too. The big flash of light scared him. To Ford, it seemed to be the reason why the lights went out.

"Can it be a nuclear detonation?" Ford considered. "That wouldn't explain why the stars went out. Is it maybe a volcano? However, that doesn't necessarily explain the lights of the city going out."

All the dreams seemed very strange to Ford. He wasn't one who spent much time analyzing dreams, but he knew someone who did. "Maybe she'll know what they mean," Ford said to himself. Ford promised himself that tomorrow he would read the e-mail again and see if he could make sense of the dreams. Then he would most likely forward them on. Regardless of what he would discover, he was planning on replying to Zack, just too at least say hi.

CHAPTER 19

Nigel

Traffic on Broadway Street was becoming thick on this final morning of December. Soon the streets would be blocked off from First Avenue to Eighth Avenue in downtown Nashville. Music City was hosting a very large New Year's Eve festival with events beginning at noon. Foot traffic would increase as somewhere around five hundred thousand participants were expected by midnight. There would be food vendors and beer tents. Seasonal temperature averages were in the mid-forties for Nashville, Tennessee; but thanks to some unseasonable warm weather, the highs for the day were predicted to be in the high fifties. Weather like this would ensure a large turnout.

As far as Nigel could tell, there wasn't any suspicious police activity in the downtown area near Music City Center and the Country Music Hall of Fame. Nigel detested country music, and he would be glad to see this place go. Even before he had converted to Islam, he had thought it was just hillbilly, redneck music.

According to Ali, the bomb would destroy everything in a half-mile radius. They had hopes of destruction across the Cumberland River at LP Field as well. According to the local FEMA standard operating procedures, the NFL football stadium would serve as a shelter in case of emergency. Nigel wasn't sure how effective an open-air stadium would be for shelter in the middle of winter, but he didn't care.

Nigel turned north on to Fourth Street and continued his surveillance. As he passed Starbucks, he noticed the state capitol building on his left. It made him wonder if anyone was planning on hitting the nation's capitol building in Washington, DC. He could only hope.

CHAPTER 20

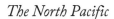

The North Pacific

Commander Vladimir of the Russian Pacific Fleet was captain of a new nuclear sub that was virtually undetectable. It was armed with the latest in Russian war technology, including the recently leaked nuclear torpedo. The torpedo had an effective launch range of about five miles, and it created a sonar signature that was far too visible. But they didn't need to get too close to prove the effectiveness of the weapon. The plan was not to blow up anything but to create a large tsunami wave that could engulf a coastal city.

Once the sub came within range of the US coastline and exited international waters, they would be at risk. With increased instability around the globe, the Americans would likely be more willing to shoot first and ask questions later. Even the current American president, who had the spine of a jellyfish, might take quick action.

The commander's mission was to maneuver to within fifty miles of the coast and launch the torpedo so that it exploded off the coast of California. The hope was that it would create such a large explosion that the resulting tsunami would decimate San Francisco.

CHAPTER 21

The Mediterranean Sea

The Chinese aircraft carrier, Shi Lang, had arrived in the Mediterranean Sea a few months ago. Since that time, it had participated in war games with the Russians and the Iranians on more than one occasion. The Mediterranean Sea was getting crowded with fleets from the United States, Russia, China, Iran, and several NATO nations making patrols. It seemed like it would only be a matter of time before some altercation potentially escalated to something bigger.

In a one-on-one scenario, the United States still held the upper hand in the Mediterranean, primarily because of their superior technology, as well as their pure numbers. But when you considered the recent collaboration between the Chinese, the Russians, and the Iranians, the Americans were sorely outgunned. Even with other NATO nations in the vicinity, there was no way that the United States could prevail.

The United States also didn't know about the presence of the secret Chinese sub that had superior stealth capabilities. Just a week earlier, it had slipped in through the Straits of Gibraltar undetected. It had nuclear capability, as well as torpedo technology, that could sink virtually any aircraft carrier in the region.

CHAPTER 22

The Caspian Sea

The Russian A-class battleship, *Stalingrad*, was on patrol about one hundred miles north of Tehran, Iran. They had gone silent only four hours earlier, at 6:00 p.m., Tehran time, and 4:00 p.m., Paris time, on December 31. The *Stalingrad* was equipped with twenty KH-101 cruise missiles, which were capable of hitting targets more than 1,500 miles away. Additionally, there were four KH-102 nuclear-capable cruise missiles onboard.

The covert CIA listening post located in Rasht, Iran, had communicated to the United States military command in the Middle East that the *Stalingrad* had gone silent only fifteen minutes after it occurred. The CIA team lead was immediately concerned about a coming attack and had voiced his opinion to his superiors. Their response was less than positive when they told him to close up shop and get to Turkey as soon as possible.

The CIA team lead had spent years infiltrating Iran to set up this listening post, and in a moment's notice, he was told to evacuate. He didn't like the sounds of that. Either it was a major screw-up on the part of Langley, or something extremely bad was about to happen.

Breaking protocol, he messaged his old boss who was stationed in Dubai. He too had been told to evacuate. Never in the history of the CIA had such drastic action taken place. He said a quick prayer and told his team that it was time to go.

CHAPTER 23

Ford

Even after staying up late the night before, Ford had awoken in time to see the sunrise New Year's Eve morning. During the last few weeks, he had been having trouble sleeping. He had slept about four hours the night before and was in desperate need of coffee. There was just way too much going on to sleep.

Ford opened a new package of coffee, and the smell of freshly ground coffee filled the room. It was a new French vanilla blend that he had been excited to try. As he prepared the coffeemaker, he contemplated Zack's e-mail and the dreams that it contained. Even his subconscious couldn't figure out what they meant, if they meant anything at all. He decided that once he was finished with his morning coffee, he would forward the e-mail to another dear childhood friend and see if she could make any sense of it.

While waiting for the coffee to brew, he decided to build another fire in the fireplace. The blanket that Abby draped over herself the night before lay on her chair. Her book was on the end table next to the chair. The previous night, before going to bed, Ford decided to wake her and have her come to bed with him. He smiled to himself at that memory. She was so funny when she was sleepy. She reminded him of a child as he led her to bed. Now Abby still slept comfortably while he began to build a fire. There still were some hot coals from the previous night, so it wasn't long before he had a nice fire going.

Ford poured himself a cup of coffee, and the rich aroma filled his nose. He walked back into the family room and sat on his chair by the fire. He set the cup of coffee down on the end table and made sure to use a coaster. Abby could be a little particular when it came to the use of coasters. He would let the coffee cool a few minutes before he tried it. While he waited, he decided to pick up the Bible. He opened the book up to the book of Matthew chapter 24. This chapter he had read many times because it spoke of the time of the end. In this scripture, Jesus shared many things about the coming end. He said that there will be wars and rumors of wars but that we should not be alarmed. He said that nation will rise up against nation. He continued to say that there will be famines and earthquakes in various places. He called all these things birth pains. Ford found the reference to "birth pains" very interesting.

Ford had always thought that there was some significance to these particular verses. Of course, everything that Jesus said was important, but Ford felt that these verses were a clue to the timing of the Tribulation. Jesus had been very clear that no one on earth or in heaven would know the day or the hour of Jesus's second coming. Only God knew. But he also said there would be signs, and those watching would recognize the coming of the end.

Ford picked up his coffee and took a sip. It was full and rich and especially delicious. He liked his coffee black so that he could experience the true flavor of the blend. Ford sipped his coffee and watched the fire for a few minutes, and as he sat there, he wondered about wars and rumors of wars.

Anyone could pick up a history book and see that humans had been at war since the beginning of time. So how would Jesus's warning of wars and rumors of wars help determine that the time of the end was near?

Ford flipped open the Bible to the book of Ezekiel. He thumbed through it until he reached chapter 36. He took another sip of his coffee and then set the cup down so that he could focus completely on the scripture. Ezekiel 36 is a prophecy about the return of the Jews to Israel. The Jewish people had been exiled from Israel for almost 1900 years. Only in the last century have they started to go back to Israel in large numbers. The largest migration of Jews back to Israel started after the United Nations reestablished the country of Israel in 1947. Ford skipped to the next chapter in Ezekiel. In Ezekiel chapter 37, there is more prophecy about the revival of the Jewish people in Israel.

Ford found it astounding that these two chapters in Ezekiel had been fulfilled in the last century. Much of the prophecy related to the time of the end relies on the return of the Jewish people to Israel. So up until recently, the wars around the globe didn't signify the birth pains that preceded the second coming of Jesus. They were simply wars. Jesus's message about wars and rumors of wars could only be applied to the time of the end, and the time of the end also relied on the return of the Jewish people to Israel. Of course, there was more prophecy that had to be fulfilled before Jesus would return.

Ford's mind brought him back to the e-mail that he received from Zack. He picked up his coffee and found the cup to be empty. He decided that he would get a refill and then go send the e-mail to Samantha. She might know what it all meant, if it meant anything at all.

CHAPTER 24

Samantha

It was just after twelve noon when Sam began to prepare lunch. She and Rob had recently returned from a short hike out in the woods. The views were breathtaking—fresh white snow, deep-blue skies, and lush green evergreens all around. The air was so clean and fresh up in the mountains Sam could stay there forever.

"Rob, lunch is ready!" Sam yelled out the door.

Rob was stacking more wood by the shed. "Thanks, babe!" Rob replied. "I'll be there in a second!"

Sam had set the table. There was a bowl of grapes that they had brought with them the day before. She had made grilled ham-and-cheese sandwiches, which was one of Rob's favorites. She had also made some homemade cheese-and-potato soup, which was another one of Rob's favorites.

"Mmmmm," Rob said with a smile as he stomped the snow off his boots. "That smells like cheese-and-potato soup!"

Sam smiled and sat down at the table.

"Sam, it looks delicious," he said as he picked up his sandwich. "Mmmmm, it is delicious," he mumbled with a mouthful of food.

Sam just couldn't stop smiling. They both seemed to be so happy at the cabin. Often she wished that they could retire and live there full-time.

Rob swallowed his food and asked, "So what do you want to do later?"

"Well, I need to call Veronica and check on Isaac," she answered. "I should also check on Jacob to make sure that he is okay."

"I'm sure they're okay," Rob said.

"Oh, I know, but I would like to hear their voices," Sam said with a smile.

The previous night, she had a dream that disturbed her a little. She figured it was nothing, but she still wanted to hear their voices. In the dream, she was watching the world from space, and in an instant, everything went dark. All the lights on the planet were extinguished. It was a short dream, but it unnerved her a bit.

"Okay, well, after you call the boys, how about we curl up next to the fire and enjoy a little alone time?" Rob said as he raised and lowered his eyebrows repeatedly.

Sam immediately smiled and mimicked his eyebrow movements. "Sounds like a date!"

After they were finished with lunch, Rob went back outside to work on the woodpile. Sam decided to deal with the dishes later because she wanted to talk to the boys and start her "date" with Rob.

Sam went into the bedroom and grabbed her phone. Her phone had five bars, and in that moment, she was thankful for cell phone service. She was about to call Veronica when she noticed that she had an e-mail. Something told her that it was important and that she needed to read it. So she opened up her e-mail to find a message from Ford.

Ford and Samantha had grown up in the same neighborhood and had known each other since third grade. Her family had moved into the house next to Ford's the summer after second grade. Sam had always been shy and was reluctant to make new friends. Fortunately for her, Ford was the outgoing type. He had come over and introduced himself the day they moved in. Sam normally would have been too shy to even say anything to him, but somehow Ford put her at ease from the beginning. That summer, there were only a handful of days that they didn't play together. They rode bikes together, they played in the woods, and Ford's dad even took them fishing a few times.

That summer, Sam fell in love with Ford. To an adult, that probably sounded ridiculous, but Sam knew that she loved him and always would. That love had grown and had changed as life moved on. Sam never really thought that it had been a romantic love. Sure, Sam had found Ford attractive, but it was his soul that she was attracted to, not his body. To most people, that probably didn't make any sense, but Sam could only describe it as a spiritual love.

Sam came back to reality and opened the e-mail.

Hi, Samantha.

It has been far too long since we've talked. I hope that Rob and the boys are doing fine. How have you been? I hope well. We have a lot to talk about, so maybe I'll call you in a couple days. It will be good to hear your voice. The main reason that I'm e-mailing you today is to forward you an e-mail from Zack. He's been having strange dreams, and I wondered if you had any idea what they might mean. His e-mail is below. Please get back to me soon. I feel like something big is about to happen. I feel far from ready, but I want to make sure that you and your family are ready too.

Take care, Sam.

Ford

PS: Happy New Year!

Sam thought about the last couple of sentences that Ford wrote. He said that something big was about to happen. Ford had always been very intuitive, and she trusted his feelings. Sam herself had also been on edge lately. Something big was about to happen, she could feel it. With that thought, Sam read Zack's e-mail.

CHAPTER 25

Christopher

It was 11:00 p.m., Paris time, on December 31, and Chris was really confused. All the chatter had stopped, and there was no evidence of any suspicious activity throughout the city. He had just gotten off the phone with Claude from the local police department, who was just as confused.

"Sara and Ed," Chris commanded, "we need to be vigilant for the next few hours. I know that we don't have the resources that are necessary, but let's do our best to stay on top of everything."

Sara and Ed both nodded in silence.

"Ed, where do we stand with the suspected cell down in Charenton?" Chris asked.

"I have nothing," Ed replied. "They seem to have gone dark since yesterday. No one has come or gone since around noon yesterday. Normally there would be continued chatter if they were going to be doing something." Ed then paused. "I'm sure we would be hearing something if there was an attack planned," he continued.

Chris nodded. It just didn't feel right. Terrorists just didn't pack up and leave. In his experience, they just didn't behave that way. They usually stayed until their job was complete, or they were dead.

"I don't like it, Chris," Ed mumbled. "I don't like it at all."

"Okay, Sara, what do you have on social media?" Chris asked.

"Well, activity seems to be about the same, but as far as I can tell, the content of the messages are all benign," Sara replied. "There was one strange post from a few days ago that has stayed with me."

Sara didn't continue and Chris could tell that she was unsure of herself. "Go ahead," Chris said. "It could be important."

"Well, it's weird," Sara replied.

"No problem," Chris said. "Out with it!"

Sara reacted with a slight jerk at his harsh words, and Chris regretted his outburst immediately.

"Well, it was short," Sara answered. "People who live in glasshouses shouldn't throw stones. That was all it said."

The team watched and waited until 2:00 a.m., and nothing happened. The entire room had just been too tense for them to even think about celebrating the New Year when the midnight hour came around. Finally, Chris told the team to get some rest. Ed didn't waste any time packing up and heading down the hall to his room. Sara seemed to be taking her time, and Chris wanted to know what was going on in her head.

"Hey, Sara," Chris started, "I'm sorry about being a little short earlier."

"Chris, don't worry about that," Sara replied. "Everything is way off, and we're all stressed out."

"Okay, I just wanted to make sure you were okay because you seem a little distracted," Chris said. "It's just that none of this adds up." Sara looked Chris directly in the eye. Her gaze was going to melt him if she didn't turn away soon. "Something is going to happen," she continued. "I just know it."

Chris nodded, and they sat in silence for a few minutes, although it seemed like an hour to Chris. In his mind, he was trying to figure out how to extend their time together. He really wasn't tired and knew that he probably wouldn't fall asleep for several hours.

"Hey, Chris?" Sara questioned.

"Yeah, Sara," Chris replied.

"I'm not really tired, and I don't think that I'll sleep tonight," Sara said with a pause. Chris could tell that she had more to say, so he waited. "Do you want to go get a cup of coffee down the street?" Sara asked shyly.

Chris thought that he noticed her flush a bit. Then he felt warmth in his face as well. He got up quickly from his chair and walked to the window. He stood there for a moment and then turned toward her.

"Sara, that sounds like a great idea," he replied with a smile. His heart began to race. He knew that this wasn't a date, but it felt like more than coffee with a colleague. "Let's go."

Chris and Sara walked out of the apartment and down two blocks to an all-night café where they had gone on many occasions. Chris held the door for Sara, just like he did on every other occasion. However, this time, it felt different.

There's no way that she likes me, Chris thought as they were seated. *She's just too beautiful. She's way out of my league.*

When they received their coffee, Chris took a moment to look at Sara. She was holding her cup of coffee with both hands, and her eyes were locked on him. Once again, he was caught up in her gaze. She continued to look at him and blew gently on her coffee; and then after a moment, with a slight smile, she lowered her eyes and took a sip of her coffee.

CHAPTER 26

Paris, France

In a vacant warehouse on the east side of Paris, the vehicles were being loaded with their cargo. There were four large dump trucks and two delivery vans. The drivers of these vehicles were in the back room, making their final preparations. Most had just finished their last prayers before heading out on a mission from which they wouldn't return. Successful or not, none of them would ever see the light of the coming dawn.

CHAPTER 27

Samantha

Samantha looked at Ford's e-mail one more time. At first, she couldn't make anything of Zack's dreams. She found it interesting that Zack was having potentially prophetic dreams. As far as Sam knew, Zack still wasn't saved, regardless of the attempts made by both Ford and Sam over the years.

She had just gotten off the phone with Veronica. She wanted to make sure that Isaac was doing okay. Isaac said that he and Joel were having fun playing video games. She hoped that they wouldn't be playing games all weekend. Sam was sure that Veronica would probably make them go outside at some point later in the day.

She decided that she would make a quick call to Jacob to check on him and then get back to Ford's e-mail.

"Hello," Jacob answered the phone.

"Hi, honey," Sam said with a smile. "How are you doing?"

"Hi, Mom, I'm doing pretty good," Jacob answered. "I was just about to go over to Travis's house for dinner. His mom said they have more than enough."

"That's nice of them," Sam replied. "Please make sure that you are home tonight by ten, okay?"

"Okay, Mom," Jacob replied, "no problem. I have some reading to do for history class anyway."

"You have a good night, sweetie. I love you!" Sam exclaimed.

"I love you too, Mom," Jacob replied. "Happy New Year!"

"Happy New Year!" Sam replied.

Sam hung up the phone with Jacob and went back to Ford's e-mail. She read it several more times and couldn't really figure out what it might mean. It was dinnertime, and she would think about it while she and Rob ate.

"Glass buildings and falling cars," she said to herself. "Well, falling things the size of cars."

Sam wondered about Zack's third dream, the one where the lights went out. Was it a coincidence that she also had a dream in which the lights went out? Her dream was more global, and his seemed to be local and only affecting one city.

"That first one definitely seems like a tsunami dream," she said aloud.

"What, dear?" Rob said from the living room.

"Oh, nothing, honey," Sam replied. "I was just thinking about a dream that Zack had."

"Zack? When did you hear from him?" he asked with some enthusiasm. "How is he doing?" He walked into the kitchen.

"I didn't hear from him," Sam said. "He apparently sent an e-mail to Ford about some dreams that he had, and Ford sent it to me. I think Zack is doing okay, though." She smiled.

Rob had always liked Ford and Zack. Both had come to their wedding and visited on occasion. All three of them seemed to get along pretty well. At first, when Sam told Rob about her two best friends, he was a little surprised that they were both male. He never asked if she had been intimate with either, and she never told him about the one kiss she shared with Ford. It was during their senior year in high school, and it didn't go any further than that, so she figured it didn't really count.

"What dreams did Zack have?" Rob asked.

"Huh? Oh," she answered and then went on to tell him about all three dreams. Rob too was mostly confused by the glass-building dream. Near the end of their conversation, she also shared with him the dream that she had the night before.

"Hmmm," Rob said. His expression had changed. He seemed to be in deep thought.

Sam wondered what he was thinking and finally asked, "What's going on in that head of yours?"

"Samantha, you are not going to believe it," Rob replied. He paused for a moment. "Last night, I had a dream just like the one that you had. That's crazy, isn't it?"

Sam didn't like the feeling that she was having in her stomach. She knew that these dreams probably meant something, and she hoped that she could figure them out before it was too late. Sam looked out the window, and the snow had just begun to fall.

CHAPTER 28

Nigel

Nigel and his team sat in their hotel room watching the New Year's festivities at Times Square on television. It was 11:30 p.m. in New York City and 10:30 p.m. in Nashville. Only thirty minutes until their bomb would detonate. They had been instructed to wait outside the blast radius until after midnight. If the bomb did not go off, they had been told that they needed to strap on vests and enter the hit zone and do as much damage as they possibly could. Nigel hoped that the bomb would go off because he wasn't nearly ready to blow himself up. He knew the other three would follow orders, and he suspected that they had been told to kill him if he didn't don on the vest. Nigel had been told to do the same to them.

Nigel stood up and went to the window. From his south-facing window, he could see the lights of the festivities going on downtown. Their hotel was on the east side of the river and close to the highway. This location made getting out of the city fairly easy, assuming everything went as planned.

Earlier in the day, Saif had suggested that they take up positions on a tall building and use their rifles to take out anyone who escaped the blast. Nigel had immediately shot down that idea. He had no desire to be trapped in a sniper hole, waiting for the cops to kill him. Slip in and slip out—

that was their goal. He had told them that they would have their chance to kill more Americans very soon.

CHAPTER 29

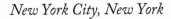

New York City, New York

The helicopter took off at 11:30 p.m. The cargo had been loaded on only forty-five minutes prior. Assif had finished flight school only six weeks before but felt fairly comfortable in the aircraft. He had been instructed to fly down the Hudson River until he reached the area known as Hell's Kitchen. Assif thought that was an appropriate name because that was where all those infidels would be eating for the rest of eternity.

Assif would use GPS to navigate through the endless corridors of buildings that made up New York City. Once near Hell's Kitchen, he would travel southeast along Forty-Seventh Street. There was a very good chance that once he made that turn, the authorities would begin to ping him. They would have little chance to stop him once he made it to Seventh Avenue. From there, he would fly southwest, low over the crowds, and detonate as soon as he reached his target. He was less than thirty minutes away from meeting his Maker, and he was about to make his family very proud because he would become a martyr for Allah.

CHAPTER 30

Paris, France

The oversized bay doors opened, and the four large dump trucks left first. The first two were loaded with C-4 explosives. They were rigged to detonate upon impact. The other two dump trucks were loaded with a blue napalm-like substance. The drivers didn't know the technology behind the explosions, but they knew in which order they were supposed to go. The C-4 would remove most of the cement and other material away from the large metal structure. Then the blue napalm would explode and heat the metal to the point where the structural integrity would be compromised. At that point, they would simply wait for gravity to do its job.

The two vans were equipped with both C-4 and the blue napalm, but they had another destination in mind. The detonation device of the first van was cleverly rigged into the air bag system. This ensured that the blast would be triggered upon impact. The second van would be detonated manually by the driver. Each vehicle was manned by two jihadists, and all twelve of them were ready to die.

CHAPTER 31

Ford

Ford and Abby decided that they would watch the New Year's Eve festivities on the television. Their oldest son, Tom, had gone out earlier and was planning to stay the night with friends. Their youngest son, John, was hanging out in his room with his best friend, Hal. They had planned an all-night video-gaming session.

Abby had just made a couple bowls of popcorn. She came into the family room with two bowls. She handed one to Ford before she sat down. On the television, the host was introducing the latest pop sensation. There were lights and pyrotechnics and a wide variety of colors and strange clothing. Ford just didn't understand the music of the day. Maybe he was too critical, but more and more, it seemed like pop stars used pagan symbology and sex to sell records.

When the musicians finished, the crowd went wild and began chanting their name. Ford shook his head and was thinking that this was a form of idolatry. He was about to suggest that they turn off the television when he felt that shudder again.

"Oh no!" Ford exclaimed. It was only minutes before the countdown would begin, and the ball had already begun its decent.

Abby looked over at him questioningly. "What is it, Ford?" she asked.

"Oh no!" he repeated. "Something is not right. I just had that shudder again."

The countdown was down to the last thirty seconds of the year.

Abby looked at Ford with some concern. "What does it mean, Ford?" she asked.

"I don't know, sweetheart, but I feel like something really bad is about to happen," he replied.

The announcers on the television were chanting the countdown with the crowd of near a million people. "Ten, nine, eight, seven…"

There was nothing that Ford could do but watch.

"Six, five, four, three…," the announcers continued. The ball had just about reached its destination when the helicopter came into view.

"Oh…," Abby started in terror. Then the scene on the television screen flashed and went blank.

CHAPTER 32

Nigel

igel and his team were watching the New Year's Eve celebration at Times Square on television. There were seconds left, and the crowd was chanting the countdown. A couple seconds before the ball reached its destination, the helicopter came into view and exploded. A split second later, he heard an explosion several blocks away. The flash lit up their room, and Nigel knew that he would soon be on his way home. The four of them went to the window to witness the large cloud of fire and debris rising up through the night sky. From somewhere in the room, he heard someone say, "It's beautiful!"

A few seconds later, the power went out. He wondered how much damage their bomb had caused and how many people they had killed. For an instant, he had a twinge of guilt, but he pushed it away.

"Let's go!" Nigel commanded. With that, they grabbed their bags and quietly left the hotel. In a matter of minutes, they were on I-65 heading north, leaving death and destruction behind them.

CHAPTER 33

Christopher

C hris and Sara had spent about an hour at the coffee shop. Chris found himself becoming relaxed for the first time in months. He sensed the same in Sara. They had come back to the apartment, and Chris had expected to go to bed. However, Sara began to open up a little bit more. She shared some information about her family and how she had wanted to make something of herself and not rely on her family's fortune. She also shared with Chris about her experience of being the homecoming queen in high school. Chris couldn't remember how that topic came up, but Sara seemed quite embarrassed about it. Chris could totally imagine Sara as a homecoming queen. The only thing missing was that she wasn't fake like most of them.

Chris looked at his watch and saw that it was almost 6:00 a.m. Even though yesterday was uneventful, he knew that they had to get back on the clock soon. He was about to suggest that they both get a little sleep when he heard the engine of a fast-moving vehicle approaching. He got to the window just in time to see a white van speeding by. The van took a sharp turn to the left and headed over the river. As the van finished its crossing, another similar van zoomed by, following the first.

Sara met him at the window and looked up to him questioningly. He met her gaze and could see the concern in her eyes.

"Go wake—"

Chris was about to tell her to wake Ed when the first explosion occurred.

The explosion seemed to have been in the vicinity of the Louvre. Seconds later, before the cloud of smoke cleared, there was another explosion. This one sounded more suppressed, as if it had been underground.

"Sara, we have to call—,"

The entire apartment was shaken by another huge explosion. The western sky lit up, and before the light faded, a fourth explosion was triggered. Chris ran to the west window of the apartment to see a cloud of smoke and flames rising around the Eiffel Tower. Before he had a chance to say anything else, he was temporarily blinded by twin explosions at the Eiffel Tower. Paris was under attack. He had to call everyone.

CHAPTER 34

Ford

Ford and Abby couldn't believe their eyes. The television screen had been blank for only a few seconds when the network switched to another camera. For a celebration like the New Year's Eve countdown at Times Square, there was guaranteed to be hundreds of cameras in play. The host of the New Year's Eve countdown was nowhere to be seen. People were running everywhere. Ford wondered how many had died from the explosion and how many more would die from their wounds. He shook his head and said a quick prayer for everyone involved.

The television showed the top of the building where the New Year's Eve ball dropped every year, and most of it was gone. It showed a large section of the ball that lay on the street. Ford remembered the helicopter and mumbled, "We are at war again."

Abby looked over to him. Her concern was growing by the second. Ford wondered if this was indeed the beginning of the events that would neutralize the United States so that it was unable to stop the Persian ram.

The news coverage continued to show the devastation as the network scrambled to get on top of the story. A few minutes later, an anchor from the news network, who was obviously distraught, shared news of another attack in

America. The anchor shared brief pictures and news about an attack that had taken place in Nashville. Apparently, another New Year's Eve celebration had been hit. So far, there were only vague estimates of casualties, but already it was clear that they would far exceed those caused on 9/11.

CHAPTER 35

Samantha

S am and Rob lay wrapped up in a blanket on the floor by the fire. Sam had earlier lit candles to set the mood. It had been a long time since she and Rob were able to spend time alone like this. Her back rested against his chest, and he had his arms wrapped around her waist. She had always wondered how it was that they could fit so well together. It was as if they weren't meant to ever be apart.

A call came in just after 10:00 p.m. Sam wanted to enjoy a little more time with Rob, so she ignored it. But when it rang again almost immediately, she knew that something was wrong. She got up and walked across the room to get her phone.

"Nice!" Rob exclaimed with a sly smile.

At that moment, Sam was reminded that she was not wearing any clothes. She looked at him and smiled while she shook her head. Deep down, she loved that he still found her attractive. She picked up her robe and put it on.

"Awww," she heard Rob say in a sad voice. She looked over at him, and he was pouting like a child. She laughed and waved her hand at him as if to tell him to stop. He laughed as well.

Sam picked up the phone on the last ring and said, "Hello."

"Veronica, wait slow down!" Sam said as she tried to calm her friend.

"Is Isaac okay?" Sam asked.

"Yes, the boys are fine," Veronica started. "But we are under attack."

"Who's under attack?"

"America is!" Veronica was almost yelling now.

"Veronica, please calm down," Sam said, trying to calm her friend. "Tell me what happened."

Sam looked at Rob as Veronica shared with her the massacres that had taken place at Times Square and Nashville. There was other news about attacks in Paris as well, but for now, there was little information about that.

When she got off the phone with Veronica, she shared everything that she learned with Rob. He seemed more concerned than she had expected. Generally, he was calm and collected, but he seemed a bit unnerved by everything.

"Samantha, I think we should pack up and go home," Rob said.

"Yes, I agree, but first let me call Jacob," she replied.

Jacob had listened to her and had been home by 10:00 p.m. He had gotten home just in time to witness the carnage on television. He seemed pretty shaken up but was ready to do whatever was necessary.

"Jacob, we don't know if there are any more attacks coming," Sam started. "Please get the go-bags ready and stay on top of the news. We should be home within an hour or so. The snow has really picked up, so it might take us longer than I think." Then she asked, "Jacob, could you also go over and pick up Isaac?"

"Sure, Mom," Jacob answered.

"Thanks, I'll just feel better if we are all together," Sam said.

"Yeah, me too," Jacob replied. "Oh, and Mom?"

"Yes, dear?" Sam asked.

"I love you, Mom. Tell Dad too," Jacob said. Jacob wasn't one to share his feelings these days, and she was grateful for this moment.

"I love you too, honey," she said with a smile. "We'll see you   soon."

CHAPTER 36

Christopher

E d came rushing in so unexpectedly that, out of reflex, Chris drew his sidearm. Ed stopped in his tracks and lifted his hands. Chris slowly holstered the weapon and apologized.

"Wow! All hell has broken loose out there!" Ed yelled over the sound of emergency vehicles throughout the city.

They had found out from Claude, their contact at the local police station, that the Louvre and the Eiffel Tower had been the only targets. Fortunately, due to the timing of the attacks, there were minor casualties so far. At the Louvre, there were only a few fatalities. Two security guards and a custodian were reported. Claude had sent them surveillance footage from the Louvre and promised some from the Eiffel Tower as well.

As far as Chris could tell, the two vans that had driven by the apartment crossed the river, took a hard right over the curb, and then accelerated all the way to the glass pyramid. The initial impact of the first van against the sloped wall of the pyramid sent a storm of glass particles into the air. A split second later the device that was in the van exploded, sending glass and debris hundreds of feet away. One camera angle caught the initial flight of the vehicle after it hit the pyramid. The short ledge that surrounded the pyramid acted like a ramp, launching the van at an angle upward and toward the pyramid. That camera was destroyed by the blast that followed. Seconds later, the other van was captured by secondary cameras around the perimeter of the pyramid. With the integrity of the glass pyramid destroyed, the second van simply vanished into the hole left by the first blast. A moment later, the second van exploded several floors below the street's surface, resulting in a complete collapse of the pyramid and surrounding structure. The plume of smoke could be seen for miles. The damage to the Louvre was irreparable, and Chris could only imagine the millions or billions of dollars lost in rare paintings and artwork.

"I can't believe it," Sara said under her breath. "All of this happened right under our noses." She cradled her face in her hands.

Chris could hardly believe it himself. He put his hand on Sara's shoulder, attempting to reassure her.

After a moment, he removed his hand from Sara's shoulder and walked to the window. The area around the Eiffel Tower was still in flames. In all his years, Chris had never experienced anything like this. It was difficult to know where to start.

"Ed, see if you can get Claude to give you some backup and head down to that location in Charenton that seemed to go silent recently. Let's see if we can find anything down there," Chris commanded.

"Roger that," Ed said and started for the door. At that moment, Chris's phone rang, and he motioned to Ed to wait for a moment. It was Claude, and he had a report on the Eiffel Tower. After a moment, he waved off Ed so that he could get to work.

Sara sat at her computer checking all her social media sources, and everything was quiet except one. The same one that had the cryptic post about glasshouses had another interesting post, and it said, "How resolute are you, sitting alone at your desk?"

When Chris hung up the phone, Sara didn't waste any time. "Hey, Chris, check this out!" Sara exclaimed.

She showed him the quote. He said nothing but immediately called Langley. He was only on the phone for a short time, but when he hung up, he plopped down on his chair and exhaled loudly. He leaned forward and put his elbows on the desk. He sat there with his hands shielding his face for the longest time. Sara sat there watching him and wondered what was going on in his head. She noticed that he had a touch of gray at his temple. She didn't care that he was fifteen years older than her; there was something about him that she found really attractive. At six feet, he was slightly taller than average. For a guy who had recently turned forty, he sure kept himself in shape. He was a good-looking guy, but there was something else that attracted her.

Confidence, Sara thought. Yes, it was his confidence that made her squirm inside. She had to hold back a smile from her thoughts. *How can I be thinking like this after what has happened?*

Chris removed his hands from his face and looked over to Sara. She seemed to be dealing with some internal struggle. Neither of them had time to deal with any personal issues. He was about to say something when she looked up at him. Once she realized that he had been watching her, she immediately flushed.

Hmmm? Chris thought. Then he pushed those thoughts away and started telling Sara the situation at the Eiffel

Tower. "Sara, it's not good," Chris started. "Apparently, there were four explosions at the tower. The devices were directed at the south and west legs of the tower. The first explosive seemed to be meant to destroy cement and other surrounding material while the second blast was meant to create extreme heat. Firefighters are currently putting out fires all around the tower.

"Right now, it is unknown if there are any fatalities at the tower. There is so much debris. Some of it was found near a soccer field that is a couple blocks away. There is some concern that the heat created by the second set of blasts has degraded the integrity of the steel that makes up the legs of the tower. They have ordered a survey to be completed as soon as the fires are put out and a perimeter is erected around the affected area."

Chris continued with the assessment for a few more minutes and ended with the revelation that there was a chance that the tower might fall. "They said that they would send over surveillance footage as soon as possible," Chris said.

A few hours later, word came to them that ISIS had taken responsibility for the attack, as well as a couple of attacks that had taken place in the United States. Apparently, these attacks were in retaliation for the most recent bombings conducted in Syria by the Americans and the French. Chris and Sara couldn't be concerned with the attacks on the homeland just yet; they had enough to deal with right in front of them.

"Well, it seems like we know what that post about glasshouses means," Sara said.

"Yeah, and now I wonder what that other post means," Chris questioned. "It sounds like Langley has notified the

Pentagon, but who knows what they'll do with it? Let's go down to the Louvre and see if we can discover anything new."

CHAPTER 37

Ford

It had been late when they went to bed the previous night. The television was dominated by news of the attacks in New York City, Nashville, and Paris. The casualty count in Paris was very limited, but in New York City and Nashville, they were catastrophic. The current count of fatalities in New York City was over eleven thousand. In Nashville, it was somewhere around four thousand. There were thousands more who were injured. Never in the history of the United States had there been so many casualties due to a terrorist act.

Congress was already calling for more bombing runs in Syria and Iraq. The president, in the last year of his term, could do nothing to block their demands. With an upcoming election, his party was sure to lose if he continued to be soft on terrorists.

By 10:00 a.m., January 1, the news spread that the Eiffel Tower's collapse was imminent. Abby earlier remarked about the trip that they had taken to Paris many years ago. She lamented the fact that the tower might fall and that she had never gone back.

Tom came home shortly after 11:00 a.m., and that made both Abby and Ford feel better.

"Tom, I would like you to help me with a couple of things this morning," Ford said.

"Okay, can I take a quick shower first?" Tom asked.

After Tom had a chance to clean up and get some food in his stomach, the two of them took both vehicles into town to fill up on gas. Ford also brought half a dozen five-gallon gas tanks that he filled up and would use for emergencies. They also did a little shopping. They picked up some water bottles as well as some additional toilet paper and other essentials for storage. These items would augment what they had already stored.

Ford and Abby had been storing food for the last several years in case of emergency, and it seemed to Ford that an emergency might come on the heels of these attacks. Ford estimated that they had enough food for the four of them to last almost seven years. Ford hoped that it would be enough.

CHAPTER 38

Samantha

S am hadn't realized how much snow had fallen in the last several hours until they started clearing off the Jeep. It had taken them about forty-five minutes to get the camp cleaned up and get everything packed into the vehicle. They decided that they would come back next weekend and do a more thorough cleaning. Rob's parents would understand, given the current state of the nation. Sam guessed that they had already gotten six inches of snow in the last couple of hours. She was beginning to get concerned about the driving conditions. Rob reassured her that everything would be fine.

The first few miles went slow on the curvy mountain road. The snow was still falling, and Sam guessed that they had another ten miles to go before conditions would improve. She figured the snow would eventually turn to rain, and they would be in the clear. Five minutes later, all those feelings would change. As they came around the last hairpin turn on the descending mountain road, they hit a large drift. Rob had become confident in the Jeep's ability to drive through almost anything, and it was likely that that confidence was misguided. When they plowed into the drift, the Jeep was pulled to the right and toward the side of the mountain. Rob overcorrected and put the vehicle into a spin.

Sam screamed as they slid out of control. She looked at Rob in fear as the Jeep slid toward the edge of the mountain.

CHAPTER 39

Zack

The forest trail was quiet, and the snow began to fall harder. Earlier, Zack had decided to take a walk to the lake to see if it was frozen yet. The lake was almost two miles away, and it made for a great hike. Since the snow had been light, the hike went faster than he expected. He loved seeing birds and small animals on his hikes. Every time he went for a hike, he was reminded why he had moved to Wyoming in the first place. He found the lake to have a small glaze of ice on its surface. Zack expected the ice to be more solid in the coming days and weeks.

The rest of the hike was uneventful, and when he got to the cabin, he decided that he would check to see if he had any e-mail. It had been a couple of days since he e-mailed Ford, and normally he would reply in a few hours. However, this time, he didn't replied right away. It was New Year's Day, and he had hoped that he would hear something from his friend pretty soon.

When he opened his e-mail, he was disappointed to find that he had only received junk mail. Zack almost turned off the computer, but at the last second, he decided to check the news. The news websites were flooded with stories about the terrorist attacks in the United States and Paris. The casualties in New York alone were staggering. The fatality count in New York alone was now 12,547.

"Holy crap," Zack said aloud. He continued to surf the Internet for more information on the attacks. This was one of the times when having a television would have come in handy.

"How does something like this happen?"he asked himself.

After a short time, he got some of the details on the Paris attacks. He found the attack on the Louvre to be the most disturbing because the most prominent building at the Louvre was a glass pyramid. There was a video on the Internet showing two vans flying through the air. The first smashed the glass; the second destroyed the interior of the museum.

"Is it possible that I saw this attack coming?" he wondered to himself. "If so, does that mean that my other dreams will come true as well?"

CHAPTER 40

Christopher

The Louvre was surrounded by police and firefighters. It took some convincing for the French authorities to let Chris and Sara near the building. When they finally got past the perimeter barriers, Chris's first reaction was, "Look how big that hole is!" Apparently, he had said that out loud because Sara exclaimed, "I know!"

When Chris first arrived in Paris, he had spent some time familiarizing himself with the popular landmarks that dotted the city. He had been especially interested in the Louvre. Not only was the architecture interesting, but the contents of the museum were incredible. He had never been much of an art guy, but after taking a tour of the Louvre, he understood why art was such a big deal. He wondered how many priceless paintings and artifacts had been lost.

"I can't believe what they've done," Sara exclaimed.

"It's impossible to comprehend, isn't it?" Chris replied.

"I had wanted to get down here and check out the museum," Sara said. Chris could hear the disappointment in her voice. "But I guess that's not going to happen now."

They walked up to the hole in the ground that had once been the glass pyramid and peered over the edge. As far as Chris could tell, the hole went down almost five stories. There was no telling how much damage had been caused by the two blasts. Chris heard that the main lobby below the base of the pyramid was completely destroyed. The floors below the main lobby were primarily used for maintenance and storage of artifacts.

Chris turned away from hole and looked toward Sara when his phone rang. Sara was staring at the hole in disbelief when she finally looked up at Chris.

"Are you going to answer that?" Sara asked.

"Oh yeah," Chris said distantly. "Hello!"

"Chris, this is Ed," Ed started. "You have to come down here right away. I think we have the information that we need."

After a few minutes, Chris hung up with Ed, and soon he and Sara were on their way to Charenton.

"So what did he find?" Sara asked.

"Well, I'm not sure," Chris started. "But it sounds like he had some evidence regarding who executed these attacks. That was pretty much all he would say."

The ride to Charenton would normally take about fifteen minutes, but today Chris expected it to take two to three times that. The French authorities would have everything locked down by now, and it would be difficult to travel for the next several days.

As they drove, Chris thought about everything that had taken place over the last couple of weeks. He was trying to mentally put all the puzzle pieces together, but there were too many missing pieces to have any idea who was behind these attacks. Sure, ISIS had taken responsibility, but Chris needed to find out who had planned these attacks. It was clear that the terrorists who executed the attacks were all blown up with their cargo, but finding the mastermind was currently at the top of Chris's list.

CHAPTER 41

Copenhagen

The plan was to hit the United State's financial markets shortly after the terrorist attacks were executed. The plan was to crash their markets the day after the markets reopened. With New Year's Day being on a Sunday, Monday would be the next business day. However, Frederick knew there was a chance that the market wouldn't open Monday because of the terrorist attacks. Regardless, he was ready to execute the plan.

The final code was ready to be deployed. They would piggyback a piece of malware that had been deployed a few days ago. As far as they could tell, the malware had gone unnoticed. This particular piece of malware would allow Frederick and his team to upload whatever type of virus they pleased. The virus that Frederick had developed would cause most sectors in the New York Stock Exchange to crash. Years ago, computerized buy-sell rules ran out of control and caused massive losses in the markets. As a result of that crash, the New York Stock Exchange developed a system that would halt trading if computer orders started running out of control. This software gave traders a chance to make corrections to orders so that losses could be curbed. Interestingly, that same software blocked out of control gains. Frederick's virus would block those safeguards and allow his team to do whatever they wanted.

As a side project, Frederick had also deployed the malware to the German, French, Japanese, and Chinese stock exchanges. Frederick planned to bring down the largest economies of the world. Chaos was always his goal, and most of the time, he was successful.

Chapter 42

San Francisco, California

Vladimir held no ill will for the Americans. He was simply doing his job. He had successfully maneuvered the Russian sub within range of the American continent. He was just waiting for the command to launch the torpedo that would destroy San Francisco. For a brief moment, he was distraught by the sheer number of people who would perish if he was successful in his mission, but then he remembered that his family would probably be killed if he didn't execute the orders that he was given.

The Kremlin had made it standard operating procedure to threaten the lives of family members when certain types of missions were commissioned. They believed that threats were the only way to ensure that the orders were completed.

Vladimir had been provided additional details regarding the entire plan to destabilize the United States. His attack would induce terror. Other attacks would destroy financial markets, and even others would take out various power grids. Several papers had been written in Moscow regarding the effects of destroying the power grid in America. Some said that it would have the effect of reverting the United States back to the 1800s, but many others said that it would be worse. In the 1800s, most people provided food for themselves, and they were accustomed to not having electricity.

The United States today would erupt into utter chaos without power. Without power, gas stations would not be able to pump gas. Without gas, trucks would not be able to deliver food. Grocery stores would be emptied within the first week after the power went out. Municipal water supplies would not be able to deliver water without electricity. Without food and water, the masses would go into a state of hysteria. An estimated 90 percent of the population would die without power in the first six to twelve months.

The thought of more than 250 million people dying made his stomach turn. It made what he was about to do seem like nothing.

CHAPTER 43

South China Sea

The Chinese began raising the man-made islands in the South China Sea a couple of years ago. The rate at which they grew was beginning to alarm the rest of the globe. Already, they had built a runway that would support all but the largest Chinese military aircraft. These islands would give China a tactical advantage in the South China Sea.

The *USS Ronald Reagan* Carrier Strike Group patrolled south of Japan with Commander Hollander at the helm. A message had just come in, ordering the fleet to move into the South China Sea. Hollander didn't show his concern that the world was on the brink of war. He knew that it was his job to protect hundreds of millions of civilians back home in the United States.

Several months ago, a United States warship sailed within miles of the new island in what the Chinese called a "provocative" act. China had threatened the United States to stay out of their way, but nothing had materialized out of that dispute so far.

The fleet had received news about the New Year's Eve attacks that occurred in the United States and Paris. The world was now on alert, and tensions were rising. Hollander guessed that those attacks were only the beginning, and he wondered how long until foreign governments got involved. NATO and Russia were already at odds with the increased number of battlefield near misses in the Middle East.

So far, China stayed out of the conflict in the Middle East. They sent an aircraft carrier group to the Mediterranean several weeks ago, but command said that it did not engage in any missions within Syria or the surrounding airspace. The Chinese said that their aircraft carrier was there to support Russian interests, but Hollander wasn't convinced.

On the other hand, Chinese naval activity increased in the South China Sea. The new islands seemed to have become a staging area for some of the Chinese military. Recent recon missions had identified installations of both land-to-air and land-to-sea missile systems on the islands. It seemed that the Chinese were preparing for something.

CHAPTER 44

Sea of Japan

ccording to US intelligence, a fleet of six Romeo-class submarines left the North Korean naval base of Ch'aho a week before the New Year. Ch'aho was a submarine base located on the east coast of North Korea, about fifty miles northeast of Hamhung. The Romeo-class subs were a Russian design built by the Chinese. They had an effective range of nine thousand miles. Subsequent reports told of the submarines heading past the southern coast of Japan. From there, it was told they began an easterly course. A few days later, they were spotted a couple hundred miles east of Japan; and shortly after, they were lost.

On January 2, a fleet of frigates and battle cruisers left the main base in Haeju Bay and headed south. Both South Korea and the United States watched them intently. The same day, South Korea reported an unusually large amount of troops moving north of the demilitarized zone. In response to these provocative actions by North Korea, South Korea raised their readiness level to the second highest level.

The United States responded by deploying a strike group that consisted of two destroyers, two cruisers, three attack submarines, and one ballistic submarine into the East China Sea. These vessels had just been at port in Sasebo, Japan. Their primary mission was the defense of South Korea and

Japan. With the *USS Ronald Reagan* Carrier Strike Group heading south, the US Navy would be stretched thin. Still they out-powered all other foreign powers in the region.

CHAPTER 45

Samantha

S am awoke and, at first, didn't know where she was. She was leaning against the window of the Jeep. After a few moments, she began to remember hitting the guardrail. The Jeep lay on its side somewhere on the mountain. They fortunately hit the rail right before the scenic overlook because the land jutted out just enough to keep them from falling off the mountain. The Jeep was no longer running, but the headlights were still on. The interior lighting was dim, but she could see a little.

Her head hurt, and she felt a liquid on the right side of her face. She hoped that she wasn't hurt too badly. She turned her head to her left and saw a vague image of Rob hanging above her. He wasn't moving, and hopefully, he was only unconscious. Rather than attend to him immediately, she wanted to make sure that the Jeep was secure. She had difficulty looking out the front windshield because it was dark and because of the series of cracks that spread throughout the window. However, the headlights gave enough light that she could tell they were on solid ground. A few dozen feet in front of the Jeep, she could see more guardrail.

Sam unbuckled her seat belt and moved to attend to Rob. Movement was somewhat limited. She would either need to break out the windshield or go out the driver-side door. Rob currently blocked that door, so she decided that she would try to wake him.

"Rob!" Sam said in a loud voice. "Rob! Wake up!" She knelt on the passenger-side door and attempted to lift up a little to see if he had been hurt. She couldn't tell, but she thought that he might have blood on the left side of his face. He probably hit his head on the side window just like she had.

"Rob, honey! Wake up!" she said louder. She reached up to grab his shoulder and shook him lightly. She didn't want to move him too much in case he had a back injury. She was having trouble waking him, so she attempted to stoop inside the Jeep to better assess his condition.

She leaned past him and turned on the interior lights. With her head next to his, she said his name again. To her relief, he was still breathing, but it didn't bode well that he was still unconscious. She could see blood dripping down the side of his face. The sight of that scared her to the bone. She needed him to be okay. She said a quick prayer for him, asking Jesus to make sure that he was okay and that they would soon get home safely.

Then she remembered her cell phone. She checked her pockets and couldn't find it. Normally she would have left it in the console between the two front seats. If that was where she put it, there was no telling where it was now. Fortunately, all the windows were intact, so it was probably still in the vehicle.

The interior lights provided enough visibility for her to find it in the backseat. She struggled to reach it, and when she did, she hoped that it would still have a signal. She clicked it on and was relieved to have several bars.

"Oh, thank you, God!" she said.

She dialed 911 and was almost immediately connected to a person. She had trouble telling them exactly where they were, but the dispatcher told her that they could use GPS to track her phone. Never had she been so thankful for technology.

CHAPTER 46

Ford

It had been three days since the attacks on America and Paris. The media said that no concrete leads had been found but that the FBI and Homeland Security were working diligently to get answers.

Ford was surprised that he hadn't heard back from Samantha yet, so he decided that he would give her a call. She answered the phone on the second ring. She immediately apologized for not getting back to him and explained that she and Rob had been in an accident.

Ford was relieved to hear that they were both okay. Rob suffered a concussion along with a broken clavicle and was still in the hospital. It sounded like he would be there for a few more days while they monitored him for additional head injuries. She only suffered minor bumps and bruises.

Sam was important to Ford. He had known her most of his life. When he first met her, she had been so shy. She had a sense of vulnerability, yet as a grown woman, she had become strong and independent. Ford knew that he loved her since shortly after meeting her. It wasn't a romantic kind of love; it was more of a spiritual love. There wasn't an easy way to describe it. At one time, he thought that he felt romantic love for her. In high school, both of them decided that they would try going on a date. The date wasn't much different from any other time they spent with each other. But there was a sense of awkwardness throughout the night. Ford always found her attractive, and she always had a fair number of other guys who showed interest.

<hr />

One night before they planned their date, Sam complained that she could never get a date because everyone was afraid of Ford.

"What are you talking about?" Ford recalled saying.

"No one will ask me out because they think we are going out," Sam replied.

"Seriously!" Ford said. "What the heck! Sure, we spend a lot of time together, but it's not like we are always hanging on each other." Although, he hadn't been very sure about that. They were obviously close, and he never worried about casual contact with Sam like he would have with other male friends of his. He could hug her or put his arm around her. He would never have behaved that way with another guy.

"Maybe we do look like we're going out," Ford said. He went on to explain what he had just been thinking.

"I guess, but all my friends know that we're not going out," Sam replied.

"I never talk about you with the guys," Ford started.

Sam frowned.

"I mean, I never say anything about us not going out. And they never ask me about you. I guess it's like they all just assume we're dating," Ford said, almost to himself.

They stood there in silence for a while, and then Sam said, "Maybe we should try it."

"Try what?" Ford asked.

"Going out, silly," Sam said. Her face immediately flushed, and she turned away.

"Uh…," Ford started.

"Oh, never mind," Sam mumbled.

"No, it's just weird. I just never really thought of you that way," Ford said.

Sam whipped her head around and stared at him with her hands on her hips. "Well, why not?" she demanded. "Aren't I cute enough for you?" Her anger started to subside. Her shyness turned into insecurity as she entered high school, and the fact that no one would ask her out only intensified that insecurity.

"Dude!" Ford started. "You are beautiful! You are amazing!" He raised his voice, "Any guy would be lucky to go out with you!"

"Dude?" Sam asked and then laughed. "You are so funny, but thank you. I find it hard to think of myself as beautiful, let alone amazing." She turned away from him and looked out the window.

Ford came up behind her and put his hands on both her shoulders. She twitched slightly when he touched her. He pulled her a little closer and whispered. "You are beautiful."

She turned to him with a smile. "Thanks," Sam said, but she started to feel awkward. "So are you going to ask me out or what?" she said jokingly.

"Samantha, will you give me the pleasure of going out with me this coming Saturday?" Ford asked.

She thought that she saw a slight flush in his face and said that she would go with him.

Ford decided that they would do it right. They would go to dinner and a movie, and he would pay for everything. On the advice of her friends, Sam decided to wear a summer dress. She even had taken extra care in her makeup and hair. Ford remembered the dress being mostly blue and was very flowy. He remembered seeing her legs and, for the first time, thinking how nice they looked. She pulled back her long dark hair into a ponytail that was held up by a matching blue ribbon. He remembered noticing a lot more about Sam than he ever had before that night.

Dinner was a little awkward at first, but soon they were talking like they normally did. The movie was less awkward. Halfway through the movie, Ford decided that he would grab Sam's hand. Their fingers intertwined together, and Ford remembered it feeling good. He also remembered Sam smiling when he took her hand. After the movie, they decided to take a walk in the park. Ford pushed Sam on the swings for a while. They talked about the stars and other things. He couldn't remember everything, but he remembered enjoying the date. Of course, he also remembered enjoying every other day that he spent with Sam. They were best friends and shared pretty much everything together.

When the date was over, he drove Sam back to her house. He walked her to the front door, and all of a sudden, he became extremely nervous. He knew that the time had come for him to kiss her. She was beautiful, and she stood there looking up to him. He never realized before how much taller he was. Her brown eyes were wide with anticipation. He wanted to kiss her but was having trouble making his move. He wondered what she was thinking and almost asked. Her gaze held him like it never had before. He wondered if their friendship would be changed forever. He hoped that they didn't ruin anything.

The longer he waited, the harder it became. Then she began to smile. It was a smile that he'd seen before, but this time, it was different. With that smile, she was laughing and teasing all at the same time. She stepped up to him and placed her hands on his face. She looked at him for a brief minute more before moving in for the kiss. Ford met her partway, and when their lips met, he felt a spark. The kiss lasted longer than a peck on the cheek but not obscenely long. Ford subconsciously moved in closer and wrapped his arms around her.

The kiss ended, and both of them stood there smiling.

Wow, Ford thought. He still held a smile when Sam finally spoke.

"Ford, I had an amazing time tonight," Sam said. She leaned forward and kissed Ford on the cheek. She pulled back and released her grip on him. He almost felt as if she struggled to pull herself away.

"I'll see you tomorrow," Sam said.

"Yeah, Sam," Ford stammered, "tomorrow."

Ford smiled at her, and she smiled back as she closed the door behind her. Ford stood there looking at the door for a few moments before turning and walking down the sidewalk. He wasn't sure what he was going to do. He got into his car and sat there, wondering if he screwed everything up. For the first time, Ford had strange feelings for Sam. He recalled how her lips felt against his, how her hair smelled when he got close to her, and the way her hips moved when she walked. All these things he had seen before but really never noticed. That night, he wondered what the next day would bring. He hoped that nothing would change, but he also remembered hoping that everything had changed.

"Hey, Ford, did you hear me?" Sam said on the other end of the phone.

"Oh, sorry, I think I blacked out there for a minute," Ford replied.

"No problem. It's been a crazy few days," Sam started. "What I said is that I have had a chance to think about Zack's dreams."

CHAPTER 47

Christopher

They arrived at the warehouse in Charenton an hour after Ed called them. The entire city was shut down. The government issued a strict curfew for all nonmilitary citizens. Chris and his team would only have a few more hours before the curfew would be in effect. Ed met them outside the building, and Chris could tell that something was wrong.

"Ed, what do you have?" Chris asked.

"Well, let me show you," Ed replied and motioned them to follow. The first-floor room was filled with local police officers and other government personnel.

Ed walked them over to a closet. Behind a dresser that was in the closet, they found a secret room. In the room, the team found a map of the city stapled to the wall. Also on the wall was a largely unknown map of the tunnels and catacombs that spidered out underneath the city. There were several locations marked on the map—the Louvre and the Eiffel Tower, of course, but also several government buildings and a few churches. The national stadium of France was marked prominently, as were several large shopping centers.

Ed said that, in addition to the maps, they found other evidences that the attacks on the Louvre and the Eiffel Tower had been planned in that room. Other than the maps on the wall, the room was pretty sparse. There was a table and chairs in the middle of the room. Against one wall, there was an old bookshelf. It contained books on everything from bomb making to gardening. To Sara, that was an interesting combination. She was about to pick up the book on gardening when she noticed something on the floor. She stooped down and discovered a very small piece of paper lying under the bookshelf. She attempted to pull the paper out but couldn't without ripping it. She stood up and began pulling the bookshelf away from the wall so that she could grab the paper when Ed yelled, "Stop!"

Sara froze in place. She wasn't sure what Ed was yelling about.

"Stop, Sara," Ed said again. He started walking toward her.

"What's wrong?" Sara asked. As Ed approached her, she could see that he was looking at something on top of the bookshelf.

Ed grabbed a chair and placed it next to the bookshelf. He stepped up on the chair and looked at the top of the bookshelf. He looked a little concerned, and then his eyes lit up. "Sorry, I thought that was a trip wire," Ed said.

Sara's eyes widened. "Oh my gosh, I'm sorry," Sara said.

"No, no worries," Ed said. "It was my bad. I overreacted." With that, he grabbed something that was on top of the bookshelf and pulled. Immediately, the bookshelf slid to the left, exposing a hole in the wall.

Sara could see stairs going down and also noticed that the paper that she originally tried to retrieve was free to pick up. The writing was French, which she had no trouble translating. It seemed to be a coded message. Chris came over to check out the staircase when he noticed the paper in Sara's hand.

"What's that?" Chris asked.

"It is a coded message," Sara replied. "Without the cipher, it's meaningless to me, but maybe the locals have decoded messages of this type in the past. I think we should get it to Claude." She handed it to Chris.

"I agree," Chris said as he examined the note.

"Hey, there's a light switch here," Ed said. "Wanna go exploring?" he asked with a smile.

Chris nodded, and they all drew their firearms and made their way into the dark.

Chapter 48

Washington D.C.

Jared picked up the vest and strapped it on. Ali told him that the vest had an amount of explosives equal to one hundred sticks of dynamite. He showed him how to activate the explosive that everyone was calling blue napalm. The small nine-volt battery attached to the vest held enough voltage to detonate the explosive. All he had to do was press the green button to arm the vest and the red button to detonate it.

Jared climbed onto a van with five other men, and soon they would be on their way to the capitol building. They were making a test run for the coming day's attack. After 9/11, the number of public tours conducted of the capitol building had been limited. Every one of the men in the van had been thoroughly checked by the FBI. If you didn't pass the background check, you would not be able to take part in the tour.

Each of the men in the van was Caucasian and hardly fit the profile of a suicide bomber. However, each of these men had been harmed in one way or another by the United States government, and all were motivated to create havoc.

Ali told Jared shortly before he had gotten into the van that there were at least four other teams that had missions to execute today. The sheer number of people who would die today was difficult to comprehend. Ali said that if they were successful, then there was a good chance that the American government would not be able to function for a long time after today. Not that Jared thought the government ever functioned properly. He was just hoping to start the reboot that was necessary. He didn't believe all the jihadist crap that Ali was selling. He just wanted to make the government pay for their sins, even if the cost of that lesson was his life, along with the lives of several thousand citizens. Jared didn't follow Islam. He didn't follow any religion. In his heart, he believed that God didn't exist and that after he died, there would be nothing. He really didn't see a big difference between the life he was living and the state of nothingness.

CHAPTER 49

Samantha

Ford called early, and Sam just told him that she thought she knew what Zack's dreams meant. She and Ford both agreed that the dream about glass buildings could very well have been a premonition about the Louvre attack from New Year's Eve.

Sam suggested that the dream that Zack had about being on the beach and seeing the water recede probably pointed toward a tsunami somewhere. Ford agreed with her, but they really didn't have any more information that would help them know where.

"The only thing that I can think of that might mean it will be in the United States is that Zack has always professed that he'll never leave the country," Ford said.

"Yes, that could be true, but we still don't have any idea where," Sam replied.

"I'll contact Zack and see if he can remember anything," Ford added. "What about the other dream?"

"Oh my gosh, Ford, that one scares me the most," Sam replied, "because I had another dream that was similar, except in my dream, all the lights went out around the world."

"Sam, I think it's a nuclear bomb that goes off, but what do the lights going out mean?"

"I think the lights going out could be one of two things. One, that when the bomb goes off it, affects the power grid somehow or, two, that the lights going out symbolizes—"

She paused. She was silent for a long time, and finally, Ford asked what she was thinking.

"Uh, maybe it symbolizes all the life going out in the location of the blast," Sam replied somberly.

"Oh man!" was all that Ford could say. "I wonder what the mountains mean."

"I don't know, Ford." Sam said. "I just don't know."

CHAPTER 50

Ford

After hanging up the phone with Samantha, Ford sat on his office chair staring out the window. Their conversation was very sobering. It seemed like the world was closing in on the end-times. Ford wondered if the birth pains were already happening.

He opened the Bible to the sixth chapter of the book of Revelation and began to read. For years, he'd thought that the opening of the first seal and the rider on the white horse symbolized the coming of the Antichrist. That was the most common interpretation of the rider on the white horse, but more recently, other commentators said that the rider on the white horse symbolized events that would come to pass in the time of the end. Also, most commentators believed that the seals would begin to be opened during the seven-year tribulation. However, Ford believed that the first three or four seals were actually opened prior to the seven-year tribulation and might signify the birth pains that Jesus spoke of in Matthew 24.

Ford read Matthew 24:4–8:

> Jesus answered: "Watch that no one deceives you. For many will come in my name, claiming, I am the Christ, and will deceive many. You will hear of wars and rumors of wars, but see to

it that you are not alarme
happen, but the end is stil
rise against nation, a
kingdom. There wi
earthquakes in various
beginning of the birth

Then Ford turned to Revelation 6, which
about the first seal and a white rider bent on conquest. Ford
wondered if that corresponded with what Jesus was saying
about those claiming to be him.

Next, Ford read about the second seal and a red horse. It
is said that that rider will take peace from the earth. Ford
wondered if that corresponded with what Jesus was saying
about nation rising up against nation.

Then Ford read about the third seal and a black horse. Its
rider had a set of scales in his hands, and it is made clear that
wheat and barley, and probably most other grains and
foodstuffs, would be scarce and expensive. Ford thought that
maybe this corresponded with what Jesus was saying about
famine.

Ford flipped back and forth between the two sets of
scriptures, and it seemed like an impossible coincidence. He
concluded that at least the opening of the first three seals
would happen prior to the seven-year tribulation and would
be part of the birth pains.

Ford needed to share this with his family and friends. He
thought about the sound of Sam's voice when they were
talking about the dreams. She seemed so unnerved and
vulnerable. He would have to call her soon and share all the
revelations that he had discovered over the past few months.

to know that it was likely that the world was
e time of the end.

erable," Ford whispered to himself.

mantha always seemed vulnerable, and because of that,
always wanted to protect her. She had been his best friend
ll throughout high school and college. His mind began to
wander back to that day in high school when they realized
that they were not destined to be romantically involved. It
was awkward at first, but eventually the entire experience
helped them become even closer.

Ford remembered Sam coming over to his house the day
after their "date." She seemed as nervous as he felt. They sat
on the back porch in silence for the longest time. In reality, it
probably was only a few minutes; but to Ford, it seemed like
hours. Finally, Sam blurted out something very unexpected.

"I love you, Ford!" Sam exclaimed. Her face became as red
as he'd ever seen it.

"I…uh…," Ford started. He was completely thrown by
her outburst, and he was sure that he was as red as she was.
He could feel the heat building and the sweat starting to flow.

"Ford, I'm sorry," Sam started. "I mean, I love you so
much, but I don't think we are meant to be together in that
way."

Ford felt like he was caught in a storm and was being
tossed back and forth in the wind. His breath caught, and he
found himself gulping for air.

"Ford, are you mad?" Sam said.

Ford could feel his heart pounding in his chest. He didn't
know what to say. Everything that Sam said was so

confusing. "I guess, I don't understand, Sam," Ford said questioningly.

"Last night, I had an amazing time," Sam started "but we always have an amazing time. I have to tell you, thinking about the kiss causes shivers to run down my spine."

"You didn't like the kiss?" Ford asked. He was very confused. Everything seemed to be simultaneously moving in slow motion and at light speed.

Sam laughed and smacked him on the chest. "No, the kiss was amazing, too!" she exclaimed.

Ford scratched his head and just looked her in the eye. She was still smiling, and her eyes were playful. Yet she was saying that she didn't want to date him.

"So if everything was amazing, why don't you want to go out with me?" Ford asked.

"Ford, it's because you and I are best friends, and I don't ever want us to ruin that," Sam said. He could tell that she had more to say, so he waited. "Ford, we are so young, and if we date now and we screw it up, then there is a chance that our friendship will not last. There is no way that I can live without you in my life. I just can't!"

"Samantha, I feel the same way," Ford said. He could tell that the use of her full name affected her in some way. He would always wonder what she was feeling in that moment.

"Okay, so instead of dating, we are going back to being just friends," Ford said.

"Not just friends, Ford," Sam replied, "best friends! The kind of friends who will always be there for each other regardless where our lives take us."

Ford turned to Sam, and she hugged him. They held that embrace for a long time, and when she finally began to move away, he gently grasped her head in his hands and kissed her softly on the forehead.

"Hey, Samantha?" he asked.

"What?"

"I love you too!" he replied with a smile.

She smiled back at him, and after that moment, their relationship continued to grow and mature. They would forever be best friends, even though life would slowly pull them away from each other.

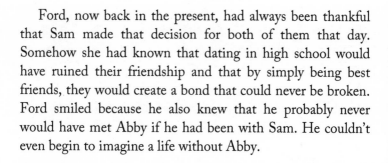

Ford, now back in the present, had always been thankful that Sam made that decision for both of them that day. Somehow she had known that dating in high school would have ruined their friendship and that by simply being best friends, they would create a bond that could never be broken. Ford smiled because he also knew that he probably never would have met Abby if he had been with Sam. He couldn't even begin to imagine a life without Abby.

CHAPTER 51

Memphis, Tennessee

Michele woke up to a shudder, which made her sit up in bed. She was somewhat disoriented and couldn't figure out what was going on. It felt as though the whole bed was sliding across the floor. She began experiencing random bouts of vertigo ever since her trip to the Middle East after her college graduation. Her vertigo was induced by an accident, and it usually occurred when her head was in an unnatural position, but it never woke her from a deep sleep. Almost immediately, the feeling subsided. She wondered if maybe it had all been a dream. The clock showed 3:01 a.m. She had four more hours before she would have to get up.

The hotel was a quaint older Residence Inn in downtown Memphis. The previous night, she marveled at the view of the Mississippi River that she had from her tenth-floor suite. At midnight, the city lights provided an interesting glow that showed on the riverboats as they made their way downriver.

Michele had come to Memphis to attend a convention on alternative learning. She had been a third grade teacher for three years and was discovering that more and more children were showing signs of learning disabilities. She read up on many topics from dyslexia to attention deficit and concluded that, with additional training, she might be able to provide better education for those being left behind. She finally convinced a reluctant school administration to let her attend this convention and bring back the tools necessary to help these children.

The previous night's speaker was very enlightening. He shared a new method for helping correct dyslexia. Michele learned that dyslexia wasn't necessarily a handicap but more like a special skill of perception. Many dyslexics had the ability to perceive things from different spatial reference points. This gave them an interesting perspective on life, but if they didn't have the tools to control this perspective change, they could have difficulty with reading and other learning. Michele was amazed to find out that a person with dyslexia would see a *b* instead of a *d* because they were simply looking at the letter from the opposite direction. This concept blew her mind.

She laid her head back down on the pillow and reluctantly decided that she would go back to sleep. She was so fascinated by everything that she had already learned. She closed her eyes, and the room began to move again.

"Crap!" she exclaimed.

Her vertigo was back. She sat back up and realized that it was something more than vertigo when the television slipped off the dresser and onto the floor in a crash. She looked at the curtains, and they were swinging as if blown by a strong wind. The final piece of the puzzle was when she saw the chair by the desk begin to hop up and down on the floor. That was when she realized that she wasn't experiencing vertigo. She was in the middle of an earthquake.

CHAPTER 52

Santiago, Chile

D r. Stephen Weinstein, of the United States Geological Survey, arrived in Santiago three weeks ago after the Chilean government notified the USGS that earthquake and volcanic activity on Mount Tupungatito had suddenly increased. They experienced a swarm of more than thirty volcanic earthquakes over the previous two weeks. Tupungatito had been dormant since 1986. The volcano historically was an explosive one, although most of the eruptions in the last hundred years were somewhat minor. Weinstein and his team believed that the high number of volcanic earthquakes in the region seemed to point to a more intense eruption in the future.

Weinstein's team was monitoring the volcano from a remote location on the eastern edge of the city. The next day, they planned to move closer to the mountain. There was a small mountain village on the banks of the Rio Colorado that would serve as their next monitoring station. That was about as close as they would get. It would take them a couple of days to traverse the rough roads into the mountains. Weinstein considered enlisting local arrieros (cowboys) to help them get closer but decided it wasn't worth it. All signs pointed to a larger explosion, and it was probably not a good idea to get too close.

CHAPTER 53

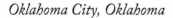

Oklahoma City, Oklahoma

Roger Steel had been in the oil business for as long as he could remember. He started Steel Oil thirteen years ago when he was forty-five. At that time in his life, he was just tired of working for the man. He decided that it was time for him to be the man. He enlisted a venture capitalist friend of his to help him get started and finally bought him out three years ago. Roger was now the sole owner of Steel Oil. Five years ago, he invested heavily into newer fracking technologies; and two years ago, his investment finally paid off. Many of the big oil companies moved into the fracking business as well, but their massive overhead reduced their profit margins. Roger ran the company efficiently, and Steel Oil was very profitable, despite the current cost of oil being low.

In light of the terrorist attacks in New York, Nashville, and Paris, oil prices were still relatively low. The low prices didn't bother Roger too much because he knew that even at $35 a barrel, his company would still be profitable. Although, $50 a barrel would be a lot better than the current price of $41. With all the unrest in the Middle East, he expected prices to creep up soon. The good thing for America was that oil production in the United States had increased to the point where the country was hardly reliant on importing oil from other countries. The only thing that would cause oil prices to go up drastically would be a complete stoppage of oil production by the Saudis, and Roger could not imagine a world where that would ever happen.

His office was based out of Oklahoma City, but most of his fieldwork was done northeast of the city. The company currently had five active fracking operations, all of which were running at 85 percent productivity. Steel Oil recently moved its offices into the First National Center building on the corner of Robinson Avenue and Park Avenue. Roger was looking out of his twenty-first-story office window as the sun was going down. He could just see the sunset between the other high-rise buildings.

As he turned to his desk, he missed a step and stumbled forward. He was able to catch himself before hitting the ground by reaching out for the desk. Lately, he was less sure of his step, and it was beginning to anger him that he was getting old. He continued to steady himself as he made it to his chair. After he sat down, he realized that the room was still moving. His stapler slid off the desk, and a frame containing the first dollar that he ever made fell from the wall in a crash. He placed his hands on the desk as he attempted to center himself. He realized that the misstep hadn't been his fault but the fault of the earth moving below his feet.

Still in his chair, he turned to the window. He could see a slight wobble in the glass and a sway of the building across the street. This wasn't a major earthquake, but he guessed that it was above 5.0 on the Richter scale.

After a minute, the world around him became still. He had experienced a few earthquakes over the past several years because there seemed to be more activity recently. Of course, the liberal fatheads blamed fracking, but Roger felt pretty confident that all the evidence pointed to something else. The earthquake activity around the world had simply increased, and that was enough for him.

CHAPTER 54

Christopher

The stairway led to an old abandoned catacomb under the city. Paris was known for its vast labyrinth of tunnels and catacombs. The catacombs were the resting place of over six million Parisians. Parts of the catacombs had been turned into a modern day-museum, but much of the tunnel system was abandoned centuries ago. Chris wasn't aware of any maps that existed showing a complete view of the underground system. Throughout history, various groups used the tunnels to serve their purposes. During World War II, the French Resistance that fought against Nazi Germany's occupation of France used them to move throughout the city undetected.

Chris and his team were in the tunnel system less than fifteen minutes when Chris stopped them.

"Guys, we need a map or a guide before we go any farther. Otherwise, the only end I see to this is us getting lost and never coming out," Chris said.

"Yeah, I agree," Sara said. "I've heard these tunnels go on forever." They stopped in a small twenty-by-twenty room that was lined with the skulls of those who had been buried there centuries ago. There was a door on each wall leading out of the room. It was almost impossible to tell which way they should go.

Ed was leaning low to the ground near the door that led to the left of the one they entered through. He seemed to be careful not to touch anything.

"Hey, boss, check this out," Ed called to Chris. Chris looked at Sara and walked over to where Ed was.

"Do you see this mark here?" Ed asked.

Chris nodded in affirmation.

"See this one here?" Ed continued.

That was when Chris realized what they were looking at. There seemed to be a hidden door just through the entrance of the door that Ed was examining. With limited visibility from their flashlights, Chris was amazed that Ed actually noticed it.

"So how do you think it opens?" Chris asked.

"Let's search the perimeter of the room and see if there is a lever somewhere," Ed answered. "I would expect it to be a manual release."

Sara came over after hearing Ed's words. "I think I may have found something over here," Sara said, "but I didn't want to touch it, in case it was a trap."

They followed her along the wall where the secret door was found. She pointed to one of the skulls that seemed to be more worn and less dusty than the rest. Ed looked to Chris and smiled.

"Good work, Sara!" Chris exclaimed.

Ed took a moment to examine the skull before grabbing it by the eye sockets and pulling downward. The skull shifted slightly out and downward before they heard an audible click in the area where the secret door was found.

Chris rushed to the door to discover that a man-sized section of the wall slid open a few inches. He pulled the door open and proceeded to enter the newly discovered tunnel. Sara followed him, and Ed came last.

The tunnel went about fifty feet before turning to the right and opening up into a large, cavernous room. As far as Chris could tell by flashlight, the room had several tables and chairs. The walls were covered with maps and newspaper articles. Sara came up next to him and flashed her light on a picture of Chris that was posted on the wall. She turned to Chris with a look of terror.

"What the heck is this?" Chris asked.

Then the overhead lights came on in a flash. Chris's eyes struggled to adjust to the light as he shielded his eyes.

"This is the end of the line is what it is," Ed exclaimed. Ed stood there holding his gun, pointing it at Chris. Chris and Sara stood next to each other with their backs against the wall. Neither of them had been prepared for this.

"What the …?" Chris yelled. "You! You're behind this?" Chris wondered how it was possible that he didn't catch wind of Ed's treasonous plan. He looked toward Sara and realized that his obsession with her had distracted him.

"Yeah, that's right Chris," Ed said as he moved around the room to achieve optimal tactical advantage. "I've been on the payroll of the Mahdi for years."

Ed's mentioning of the Mahdi put a look of terror on Sara's face. Chris didn't know what that was about, but if they made it out of here, Chris vowed to find out. Ed's smile became the look of pure evil, and Chris's stomach curdled.

"You know what I'm talking about, don't you, you little bitch!" Ed spat out.

Sara jerked back at the words as if she had been slapped in the face. Ed took a step forward toward Sara, and his face became flushed with anger. Still looking directly toward Sara, it was as if Ed transformed into the devil himself. Everything about him oozed evil.

"I'm going to kill your boyfriend here," he said, waving the gun toward Chris. "And then you and me are going to have a little fun." He pointed the gun back at Sara.

Chris was wondering if he would have enough time to draw his firearm before Ed was able to fire his. He thought if he made a move, Ed might shoot Sara. He couldn't let that happen. Chris hoped that Sara was wearing a vest.

"Oh yeah, you and I are going to have some good fun!" Ed continued as he took another step toward her.

Chris knew that he was running out of time and chose that moment to act.

Jesus, help me! Chris pleaded inside his heart. In one motion, Chris pulled his revolver and made a move to shield Sara. He pulled the trigger and heard Ed's gun go off before he fired again. The bullet hit Chris square in the chest, and as he fell to the ground, he saw Ed jerk back and fall against the wall. Ed's body rocked twice more, and then his head exploded as Sara emptied her firearm into him.

Chris lay on the ground and found it almost impossible to breathe. He still didn't know if the vest stopped Ed's bullet. He saw Sara over by Ed's body. She kicked his gun away and then ran over to Chris.

She was saying something to him, but he couldn't understand her words. His head was pounding, and his ears were ringing. Sara was tearing open his jacket and shirt. Chris looked up toward Sara, and in a moment, relief washed over her face. Her hand was on his chest, and then he saw that she was overwhelmed with emotion. She laid her head over his heart and held him tight. The top of her head was against his chin, and he could smell her hair. The smell was intoxicating. He wasn't sure if he was going to die, but in that moment, he didn't care.

"Thank you, Lord, for keeping Sara safe," he said.

Apparently, he had said that out loud because Sara raised her head and looked deep into his eyes. Her blue eyes glistened with tears, but Sara was smiling. Chris wasn't sure what was happening. Sara put her right hand gently on the side of his face and continued to smile. He was about to ask what was going on when Sara leaned down and pressed her lips against his. The kiss sent a wave of electricity throughout his body, and in that moment, he knew that he was still alive. He pressed into her, and they held the kiss for what felt like an eternity.

Sara pulled back and looked at him in a loving manner. They sure had a lot to talk about.

"Let's get you out of here," he heard her say. She got him up and into a chair.

She loosened his vest, and he could breathe much better. He would sport a large bruise for several weeks, but he would be okay. Chris sat on the chair catching his breath while Sara collected all the evidence. They didn't have any cell service in the tunnels, so they would contact the authorities to get Ed's body once they got back to the surface. Chris still couldn't believe that Ed was behind the Paris attacks. When he had a chance, he would have to ask Sara what this Mahdi thing was.

CHAPTER 55

Samantha

It had been a week since the terrorist attacks on America. Because of those attacks, the world had become more tense. Just like after 9/11, the United States government raised the threat level and increased security throughout the country. Sam wondered why they always seemed to be a step behind the terrorists. Securing the border would go a long way toward stopping terrorists from attacking the country. Neither the Republicans nor the Democrats seemed to have the wherewithal to build the fence and increase border patrols.

Living in the Southwest for much of her life, Sam knew very well that illegal aliens flooded the border on a daily basis. Up until recently, most of the illegals came from Mexico and other Central American countries. More recently, Sam recognized more people with Middle Eastern heritage in her town. She often felt bad, but she wondered how many of those people were in the country illegally.

Rob finally got out of the hospital the day before. His head still hurt, but he wasn't showing any more signs of the concussion that he suffered. Both of them were very lucky, and Sam thanked Jesus every day for keeping them safe. Today Rob was relaxing on the couch and watching television. He planned on going back to work in a couple of days, assuming that he was feeling well enough. Sam was very thankful that Rob's company was very supportive during this time of need.

"Hey, babe, can you get me a glass of water?" Rob asked.

He was in a sling because of the collarbone fracture, and the slightest movements hurt him quite a bit. Sleeping was also a problem because he was used to lying on his shoulders. He slept on the recliner the previous night because he kept wanting to sleep on his side. Needless to say, he hadn't been sleeping well.

Sam handed him the glass of water with a smile and said, "Let me know if you need anything else, dear."

Sam had to go back to work the next day and decided to sit down at the computer and see what was going on in the world. The first thing that caught her eye was Russia's increased activity in Syria. It was clear to those who were paying attention that Russia was simply filling the leadership void created when the Americans left the Middle East.

This news of Russia brought to mind a story in the book of Ezekiel chapters 38 and 39. She had been interested in Christian end-times prophecy for several years now. She and Ford held debates on many different topics. Ford was doing a more comprehensive study than Sam, but there was a lot that neither of them truly understood. She was able to convince him to change his opinion on some topics, and he had done the same for her on other topics. They both seemed to enjoy putting the puzzle pieces together.

For a long time, she considered Russia as the primary suspect of being Gog of Magog. She picked up her Bible and flipped to Ezekiel chapter 38 and read. Ezekiel 38:1-6 read,

> The word of the Lord came to me. "Son of
> man, set your face against Gog, of the land of
> Magog, the chief prince of Meshech, and
> Tubal; prophecy against him and say: This is
> what the Sovereign Lord says: I am against
> you, O Gog, chief prince of Meshech and
> Tubal. I will turn you around, put hooks in
> your jaws and bring you out with your whole
> army—your horses, your horsemen fully armed,
> and a great horde with large and small shields,
> all of them brandishing their swords."

Sam read another translation of Ezekiel that replaced the
words *the chief* with the word Rhos. Some translations have
the word Rosh.

Sam and Ford disagreed on the country that was
represented by Magog. Sam still held to the belief that it was
Russia. Ford, however, believed it to be Turkey. Sam had
been doing additional research and wanted to win this debate.
She smiled to herself when she thought about winning. Since
she was a little girl, she had always been really competitive.

Sam believed that the war described in Ezekiel 38–39 was
fought prior to the seven-year tribulation. Ford believed that
Gog was the same person as the Antichrist and that the
Ezekiel war was the same war fought at the end of the seven-
year tribulation. This debate between Sam and Ford raged on
for years. She was determined to prove him wrong on this
one.

"I will win this one, Ford," Sam said to herself with a
smile.

Sam found herself distracted by the word Rhos or Rosh.

"I guess I'll skip the rest of the world news for now and figure out what Rosh means." She found that she often talked to herself when she was immersed in this type of research.

Sam knew that many commentators argued that Rosh was a noun and that it somehow referred to Russia, but Sam really didn't buy into that translation. Others believed that Rosh was an adjective and could be translated as "chief." Sam wasn't sure which was correct and decided that she would first prove or disprove that Rosh pointed to Russia. There were four points that she thought she could use to figure this out. First, the word *rosh* should be translated as a noun. Second, the word *rosh* should be treated as the proper noun Rosh. Third, Rosh would have to be a people well-known to Ezekiel. Last, as a people, Rosh had to point to the region that was now Russia.

Sam found herself deep in thought when Rob yelled from the other room. She realized that she would have to revisit this a little later. Sam got up quickly and ran into the living room where Rob was watching television.

"There was a big earthquake near Memphis. They are saying that it was a 6.5, and it sounds like there was some damage to older buildings, but nothing too bad," Rob said. "But the reason I yelled was because there had been an earthquake in Oklahoma City as well. Apparently, there have been a lot of earthquakes lately. Most of those have been minor, 2.0s and 3.0s, but this one was a 5.3."

Sam was watching for earthquakes and volcanic eruptions lately. She knew that the numbers had been increasing over the past couple years. She wondered if this was part of the birth pains that Jesus talked about in the book of Matthew.

"Hmmm," she said questioningly, "both of those quakes were pretty significant."

"Yeah, I thought you'd find that interesting," Rob stated and raised his eyebrows. "Maybe you're right about all this end-of-the-world stuff."

Rob was a little skeptical about all her warnings. However, he did think that it was a good idea to be prepared for emergencies, so he supported Sam's quest to store food and have go-bags ready if they needed them. When she first used the term *go-bag*, she had to explain to him that it was simply a backpack that held emergency supplies and that it was ready to go at all times, in case they needed to leave in a hurry.

Sam sat down on the couch and watched more of the news. She told herself that she would get back to the book of Ezekiel after dinner.

CHAPTER 56

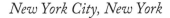

New York City, New York

A week after the terrorist attack, most of the debris had been removed. Both Seventh Avenue and Broadway were still closed between West Forty-Second and West Forty-Fourth Street. The road closures created additional traffic congestion in the area. The One Times Square building had been severely damaged when the helicopter crashed into the twentieth floor, but the explosion from the bomb had caused most of the damage. Engineers questioned the structural integrity of the building. They weren't necessarily concerned that it would fall, but it was still a possibility. They weren't sure that it could be completely repaired. Only time would tell. Regardless, it would be unusable for a long time.

The authorities had determined that the explosion was a combination of C-4 and a newer material that most called blue napalm. The C-4 did the majority of the structural damage to the building, but the blue napalm was the reason that so many people were dead. The casualty count was now 13,113. In addition to that, there were over 25,000 injured.

The explosive device was engineered to ignite the blue napalm, and the force of the C-4 was meant to launch the flaming material away from the building and onto the crowd. The resulting fireball filled the corridor along Seventh

Avenue between the buildings from West Forty-Third Street all the way down to West Forty-Fifth Street. It had also exploded back toward West Forty-Second Street along Seventh Avenue. It traveled down West Forty-Third Street, halfway to Eighth Avenue and partway to Sixth Avenue. Everyone in the immediate vicinity was instantly killed. It had taken three days to put out all the fires, and it had taken firemen from eight fire stations to complete the job. The financial losses were easily in the hundreds of millions of dollars. It was likely that it would exceed a billion dollars when it was all tallied.

Ali Basharat had instructed Assif, the helicopter pilot, on which path he should fly. Assif had executed the plan perfectly, and Ali could not have been happier. Everything was going as planned, and he prayed to Allah that the next phase of attacks would go as smoothly. The plan was to keep the United States government on its heels and the American people too afraid to leave their homes. Ali inspected each of the vests and instructed each of the twenty-four men and women on how to use them. In a day's time, the United States would truly know the meaning of terror.

CHAPTER 57

Nigel

The trip from Nashville to Washington, DC, was uneventful. The team spent most of the last few days in the hotel room and followed the news when they could. Ali met with Nigel the day after they arrived in DC and was mostly happy with their results.

The current casualty count in Nashville was 4,587, and the number of injured was over 10,000. The Music City Center was mostly destroyed, but something about the configuration of the bomb sent the majority of the explosion upward instead of outward. The majority of the roof was blown off in the initial explosion and forced the blue napalm upward and out of the building to shower down on the people outside.

Nigel thought that a configuration to blow sideways would have been more effective at killing people within the convention center. He shared this thought with Ali when they met. Ali agreed with him but had been happy with the results of the "test." Nigel looked at him strangely when he said the word *test*. Ali laughed and simply said, "Soon." That night, Ali left and said that he would be back in a few days. That was two days ago. Ali hadn't told him where he was going but he said that he had something special planned for Nigel's team.

The news coverage on the Nashville attack had talked about several country music stars who lost their lives that night. The bodies of the musicians who were playing at the time of the explosion were never found. It sounded like there were fires in as many as ninety buildings in the surrounding neighborhood. It had taken the fire department a few days to put them all out. Most of downtown Nashville was still without power.

Nigel had also heard about the earthquakes that occurred in Memphis and Oklahoma City. Ali had said that Allah was judging the infidels in this country. At the time, Nigel didn't reply, but somewhere deep inside him, he was starting to question everything that he was doing.

Nigel told his team that they could go out and get some food but that they needed to keep their heads down and not attract any attention. Nigel decided that he would stay in and watch television. He was looking around for the remote when he found the Christian Bible in the end table drawer. He picked up the book and turned it over in his hands a couple of times. Then holding the spine of the book with one hand, he fanned through the pages of the book with his other hand. The words flew past him, and in a flash, he saw the word *Jesus*. He was immediately taken aback, and then he tossed the book back into the drawer and slid it close.

CHAPTER 58

Ford

The snow continued to fall around him. Ford had decided that he needed to take a walk through the woods. He was thankful that he had decided to wear snowshoes because normal hiking would have been next to impossible in this amount of snow.

Ford had just come out of the trees and was walking up the hill toward the house when he noticed a doe standing about fifty yards away. She obviously hadn't noticed him because she was just standing there, eating the corn on the ground that had recently been dropped by the feeder that hung above her, six feet from the ground.

Ford stood there and admired her. She was a mature doe, probably four years old or so, and had a beautiful brownish-gray color. There were several deer that roamed through his property, and he probably had seen her on his various trail cameras, but he didn't immediately recognize her. He finally decided that it was time to head in and began walking toward the house.

When he neared the top of the hill, the house came into view. He looked back toward the feeder, and incredibly, the doe never moved. Maybe she knew that he was not a threat, at least today. He turned back to the house and could see the smoke rising from the chimney. He loved the smell of a fire and couldn't wait to get inside.

Before entering the house, he removed his snowshoes and stomped off his boots. He hung the snowshoes in their place in the mudroom. His boots, jacket, hat, and gloves all had their place as well.

He walked down the hall and found Abby in the kitchen.

"Hi, Ford. How was your walk?" Abby asked.

"Hi, honey. It was very relaxing," he replied. "You wouldn't believe it, but I just walked up on a doe, and she never moved. Sure, I was about fifty yards away, but normally that's close enough to spook them."

Abby smiled and then asked him what he wanted for dinner.

Ford went to his office to read while Abby was making dinner. He had been struggling with one particular part of scripture these past several days. For the longest time, he believed that Gog, who was discussed in the book of Ezekiel, was a person other than the Antichrist. He had also believed that the war that was chronicled in Ezekiel 38–39 was a war that occurred prior to the seven-year tribulation, but recently, he read a new book that might have changed his views on that.

In this book, the author compared the war described in Ezekiel with the war described in Revelation. They were amazingly similar. Ford was completely convinced that the Antichrist would emerge out of the Islamic caliphate. The questions that kept plaguing his mind were, Where was Gog from? Where was Magog?

He had e-mailed Sam several weeks ago regarding this topic. She had been a believer that Gog was from Russia.

Ford was becoming a believer that Gog would come out of the Islamic caliphate. Ford was also beginning to believe that Gog and the Antichrist were the same person, but he really needed to find more evidence before he would be able to debate it properly with Sam. Sam had replied to his e-mail, implying that she was going to do a little research herself. Of course, with the New Year's Eve attacks, neither of them had been able to focus much on biblical research.

"Ford, dinner is ready!" Abby called from the other room.

"Okay, be there in a moment," Ford called back.

Ford sat back on his chair and put his hands behind his head. He looked out the window and saw that it was snowing again. He liked falling snow. It made him feel safe for some reason. He closed his Bible and got up from his desk. He decided that he would look deeper into Ezekiel another day and maybe give Sam a call to see if she had discovered anything new.

CHAPTER 59

Mediterranean Sea

The *USS George H.W. Bush* was on its first deployment in the Mediterranean Sea. It was the newest United States aircraft carrier on the fleet. It housed over two thousand personnel and seventy-five aircraft. It was responsible for operations throughout the Middle East and Northern Africa. This modern marvel was accompanied by eight other naval sea craft, including two destroyers and two submarines. They had been on high alert since the terrorist attacks in America.

Seaman Robert Williams was an operations specialist, and his primary job was combat air control. His job was to coordinate aircraft launches and landings. For the moment, he was off duty, although you were never off duty on an aircraft carrier, especially if that aircraft carrier was in the Mediterranean Sea. He was in the mess hall getting some breakfast before his shift started.

Williams sat down at an empty table with his tray of food. The food was surprisingly good today: eggs, bacon, and toast. A large cup of coffee would top off the meal and help him get through the next ten hours of work. Everything had been extremely quiet out there the last week or so, and that was beginning to make many onboard a little anxious. Williams had been having difficulty recently because his nights were haunted by strange dreams. The worst dream was of his fiancée, Bridget, who lived in San Francisco. In his dream, he was walking up the beach and was just drying off after his swim in the ocean. He could see his fiancée across the street enjoying some coffee at a seaside café. In the dream, she saw him and waved happily. He waved back, and then the look on her face sent shivers down his spine. She stood up and frantically pointed behind him. In his dream, Williams turned around to see a massive wave coming toward him. The wave must have been over a hundred feet tall. He had no time to react, and as he turned toward his girl, the wave hit him like a freight train, and he woke up.

Back in the real world, he shook his head and took his first bite of breakfast. The eggs were good, and he reached for the bacon. That was when his world changed forever.

<hr />

The Chinese submarine had been in the Mediterranean for more than a week and still had not been detected by the Americans. For the most part, the sub stayed at least fifty miles away from the American fleet. The United States had their new flagship aircraft carrier near, and it allegedly had new state-of-the-art sonar equipment that could find even the "stealthiest" of sea craft.

This submarine's mission was to see how close they could get to the Americans without being detected. The day before, they had pressed within five miles of the fleet without detection. After pushing in so tight, they moved back out to nearly forty miles of separation from the American fleet. The commander of the vessel ordered the submarine to move to a depth where they could send a transmission.

It was around midnight when they received the reply that the entire crew had been waiting for. They were finally given the order to launch an attack on the American aircraft carrier. The entire submarine crew was at quarters, and they were in absolute stealth mode. This time, they would press to less than three miles and launch their new torpedoes. This distance would give the enemy very little time to take defensive measures. The commander's only concern was the location of the enemy subs.

The submarine *USS Missouri* was on patrol near the *USS George H.W. Bush* aircraft carrier. The last few weeks had been slow, and the crew was beginning to get restless. Everything had been quiet that afternoon until they picked up a ping. The heading was about three miles away to the northwest of their position. The operations specialist (OS) on duty immediately informed his supervisor.

"We have a trail moving at twenty-eight knots with heading of 230," the OS said.

He did the math in his head and immediately looked up to the captain and saw the recognition on his face. They knew there was a torpedo in the water. The captain quickly ordered an intercept to be launched and then placed a call to the *USS George H.W. Bush*. Based on some quick calculations, the OS knew that the aircraft carrier had just over five minutes before impact.

The interceptor was a torpedo that was meant to counter other torpedoes. In this case, it was launched a minute after the command was given, but the trajectory was such that it was unlikely to intercept in time.

The OS could track the enemy torpedo but couldn't find the sub that it came from. Their new tracking system took stealth technology into account, and with a second launch from the enemy submarine, the OS would be able to triangulate a position of the enemy. The only problem with tracking a "stealth" submarine was that they only stayed in the same position for a short period of time. Time was of the essence to counter the attack. A moment later, the OS got another ping.

"We have a second launch!" the commander heard.

"I want a fan of five M48s! Fire on their position!" yelled the commander.

Within seconds, an array of five Mark 48 torpedoes were launched toward the enemy position. They were spread out like a fan to ensure a hit on the enemy vessel.

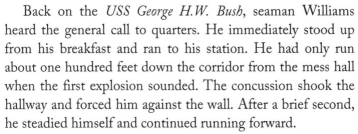

Back on the *USS George H.W. Bush*, seaman Williams heard the general call to quarters. He immediately stood up from his breakfast and ran to his station. He had only run about one hundred feet down the corridor from the mess hall when the first explosion sounded. The concussion shook the hallway and forced him against the wall. After a brief second, he steadied himself and continued running forward.

The radar technician on the Chinese submarine alerted his commander that he detected a torpedo launch southeast of their position. They were tracking five radar signatures that looked like torpedoes coming directly toward them. He knew that they were coming in from almost a ninety-degree angle, and at their current range, it would be next to impossible to avoid them.

The commander called for an emergency dive of fifteen degrees and a yaw of seventy-five degrees toward their enemy. He figured if they were able to avoid the swarm of torpedoes, then at least they might have a chance to counterattack.

The vessel dove and turned like no one onboard had ever imagined was possible, and as the enemy torpedoes closed, the commander thought for a moment that they might survive this confrontation. Then, a moment later, the command center was vaporized. A second torpedo hit the tail section as well, but the first one was all that was necessary. What was left of the submarine no longer dove at a controlled pace, and within minutes, it was resting at the bottom of the sea forever.

The *USS Missouri* was able to anticipate the second torpedo launch from the enemy sub, and the second interceptor did its job. They also detected two explosions in the area where they had fired at the enemy sub. Immediately, the enemy submarine began leaving a sonar trail as it rushed toward the bottom of the sea.

The *USS George H.W. Bush* had suffered many casualties and much damage, but it was still partially operational. Thanks to the quick-acting captain of the *USS Missouri*, they would survive this attack.

CHAPTER 60

China

Word had come to the command center in Beijing that the submarine *Wu Tow* was lost. The submarine was a big loss, but its cargo was an even bigger loss. The submarine commander had failed to launch the third torpedo, which would certainly have finished off the American aircraft carrier. The third torpedo was armed with a Russian nuclear warhead, which now lay at the bottom of the Mediterranean Sea. The Russians would not be happy, but nothing could be done about that. The aircraft carrier *Shi Lang* still had one left, and the world would soon know of the power that the Chinese military possessed.

CHAPTER 61

Caspian Sea

The Russian A-class battleship *Stalingrad* had been virtually silent for about a week. The Kremlin had sent word that the American CIA had vacated the area recently. There had been some confusion about that, but they were now ready to act.

The American air base just outside of Baghdad would be the recipient of four KH-101 cruise missiles containing white phosphorous. White phosphorous burns at about five thousand degrees Fahrenheit and was outlawed by the Geneva Convention. An airburst of white phosphorous would burn virtually everything in the blast area. In addition, two KH-101 cruise missiles containing 850 pounds of explosives each would hit the main control tower and airplane hangar.

Six more KH-101 with conventional explosives would be launched at various American positions in northern Syria. At just after sundown, the *Stalingrad* woke up and rained hell down on the Americans. Life was about to change for billions of people.

CHAPTER 62

Hawaii

The North Korean submarine fleet that had left the Ch'aho naval base two weeks before maintained position fifty miles to the west of the island of Oahu, Hawaii. Their mission was to disable the United States Pacific Fleet that remained stationed at Pearl Harbor, which was on the northwest edge of Honolulu.

Months before they left Korea, two of the six Romeo-class Russian-made subs had been equipped with the new nuclear torpedoes. The Russians provided them to the North Koreans with the condition that they be used against the Americans. These nuclear torpedoes had a nuclear warhead rated at two megatons. Because these bombs would detonate underwater, the blast radius was smaller than a similar warhead detonated aboveground. However, the primary purpose of this weapon was to create a tsunami wave that would destroy the American naval fleet docked at Pearl Harbor.

At 5:00 a.m., Hawaii time, the North Korean sub fleet came within range, and the first submarine carrying the nuclear payload launched its torpedo toward Iroquois Point on the southern shore of Oahu. The torpedo would detonate approximately three miles from the shoreline and would create a resulting tsunami wave that would be at least fifty feet high.

CHAPTER 63

San Francisco, California

Commander Vladimir of the Russian Pacific Fleet received word that he was to launch the nuclear torpedo toward San Francisco Bay at 7:00 a.m., Pacific Standard Time, and the detonation range was to be five miles from shore. This range was determined to create the most effective tsunami wave. The plan was to hit the Americans in multiple locations. In some cases, they would be conventional weapons; in others, nuclear torpedoes, such as the one that he was about to deploy.

Vladimir was given word that his submarine was now within range. The previous night, he had trouble stomaching the death and carnage that he was about to dish out, but it was time to do his duty for Mother Russia.

"Fire torpedo one!" Vladimir commanded.

In less than five minutes, the United States and Russia would openly be at war.

CHAPTER 64

Copenhagen

Thirty minutes after the New York Stock Exchange opened, Frederick deployed the virus that would shortly bring the American financial world to its knees. He also deployed a similar virus to the European and Asian markets. The events that were planned for that day would create a panic, which would cause a catastrophic crash in the American stock markets. The Asian markets and European markets would follow like dominoes falling in a row.

CHAPTER 65

Nigel

L ate the night before, Ali Basharat knocked on Nigel's hotel room door in Washington, DC. Nigel and his team were taken to a warehouse on the north side of town and introduced to their new team members. Each member of Nigel's team was paired with a drone operator and was tasked with driving a van to various locations around the perimeter of the White House. Each van was equipped with sophisticated computers that allowed a remote pilot to control multiple aerial drones. Each drone was equipped with an explosive device containing five pounds of blue napalm. There were three drones in each van that would be controlled by a separate drone operator.

Nigel was amazed by the sheer amount of explosives that would be deployed in this attack. He had been told by Ali that there would also be four other vans that would be used to breach the White House. Each of these vans contained men and women wearing suicide vests and who would soon become martyrs for Allah. There were more attacks planned for that day, but Ali didn't provide any additional details.

Nigel saluted to Ali, and he started up the van and drove out of the warehouse. Each of his team members followed in their own van. Soon Washington, DC, would be brought to its knees.

CHAPTER 66

New York City, New York

At 8:00 a.m., the NYPD received a tip that there was strange activity in an abandoned house in Brooklyn. Dispatch sent a patrol car over to the address in question. Sergeant Adam Kent and Officer Ramos Rodriguez arrived on the scene and got out of their vehicle. Sergeant Kent radioed dispatch that they had arrived on site and were going to the house to investigate. Kent went first with Rodriguez behind. Kent pushed open the short metal chain-link fence and proceeded toward the front door. Rodriguez walked along the side of the house toward the rear.

Sergeant Kent was about to knock on the door when a shotgun blast blew a hole through the door and riddled him with buckshot. He was blown back off the porch and onto the cement sidewalk. Upon hearing the blast, Rodriguez immediately called for backup and rushed to the front of the house to assist Kent.

When he got to the front of the house, he saw Kent lying on the ground. The front of his shirt was riddled with holes from what looked to be 12-gauge buckshot. It looked like his vest had stopped most of the buckshot, but a few had pierced his shoulder and thighs. None of his wounds would be life threatening, but Kent was either unconscious or just stunned. Rodriguez pulled Kent by the vest back down the sidewalk to a position behind the patrol car. When he looked up, he saw an individual running into the alley behind the house. He radioed in that Kent was down and that he was pursuing the perpetrator on foot.

As Rodriguez leaped the fence and ran to the back of the house, he heard sirens closing in on his location. By the time he got to the alley, the perpetrator was out of sight. Rather than go on a wild-goose chase, Rodriguez decided that he would go back and check on Kent. When he arrived, Kent was regaining consciousness. Rodriguez rechecked Kent's injuries just as two patrol cars pulled up.

Rodriguez gave a description of the perpetrator and the general direction where he fled, and the first patrol car drove off in pursuit. A moment later, an ambulance arrived for Kent.

The officers in the second backup patrol car, along with Rodriguez, went into the house to secure the scene. They entered through the nearly destroyed front door with AR-15s drawn. In the front room, there were a few pieces of old furniture that had seen better days, but nothing of interest there. They proceeded to sweep the rest of the house and finally came to the basement door.

Rodriguez flipped on the light and slowly proceeded down the stairs. This was the worst possible position to be in. He had virtually nowhere to go if he was confronted by hostiles. They made it to the basement floor only to find it empty of additional perpetrators, but they hit pay dirt when they discovered two dozen explosive vests. Whoever it was who shot Kent, they were planning something big.

When the bomb squad was finished with their assessment, they loaded all the explosives into their van. Fortunately, none of the vests were armed yet. They were very interested in the explosive material that made up the vests. They had heard about an explosive called blue napalm but were not yet able to get their hands on some. It was apparently a liquid that was very flammable but virtually undetectable through normal search parameters. This find would allow them to define detection methods for this new terror threat.

In Washington, D.C., Ali Basharat slammed down the phone.

"Those bloody infidels!!" Ali shouted.

He violently swept his arm across his desk, flinging everything onto the floor. He stood up and flung his chair across the room, where it shattered against the wall. It took him a moment to shake it off. New York City was important, but not as important as Washington, DC. Much damage had already been inflicted in New York, and Ali would have to be satisfied with what they had already achieved.

CHAPTER 67

Washington, D.C.

The president was in the Oval Office when he got word that the *USS George H.W. Bush* was under attack. Initial reports indicated that the attack was executed by a submarine. That could only mean the Chinese or the Russians.

The president made his way to the Situation Room, where his security council was being gathered. As he entered the room, everyone stood and waited for him to sit. He stood at the end of the table and told everyone to sit. He remained standing and wanted to know who was responsible. Initial reports were the Chinese or the Russians.

"Okay, tell me something that I don't already know," the president said sarcastically.

"Well, sir, we are getting reports that the attack sub was virtually undetectable until it launched the second torpedo," said General Joseph Adams.

Adams was the chairman of the Joint Chiefs of Staff. He was a career marine who declared no political affiliations. The president had hoped to sway him toward his liberal policies, but Adams proved to be a man of principles. He and the president had butted heads many times, but he was the most patriotic general in the United States Armed Forces. He would do anything to protect the Constitution and the people of the United States.

"We have intelligence that Russia was close to developing an advanced stealth submarine, but we are leaning toward the Chinese," Adams continued.

"Why do you think that?" the president questioned.

"We also have intelligence that the Chinese may have hacked the Russian defense department several years ago. At the time, the Russians weren't sure what information the Chinese had taken, but over time, they began to suspect they had stolen the designs for a weapon whose purpose they would not share," Adams replied.

"Okay, what word do we have from either the Chinese or the Russians?" the president asked the secretary of state.

Tyler Jameson was the youngest person to ever be appointed to the position of secretary of state. At the age of forty, he had political aspirations to become president someday, and he was willing to do almost anything to attain them.

"The Russians have yet to reply to our inquiry, and the Chinese are denying having any submarines in the area," Jameson replied.

"That's ridiculous!" the president exclaimed. "Do they think we are stupid?" the president asked rhetorically.

Yes, yes, they do, General Adams thought to himself. The general had been thoroughly disgusted with this president's political agenda. Secretly, Adams leaned to the conservative right but was careful to never share his political leanings. He had done everything in his power to subvert the president's liberal agenda without breaking the law or making his intentions clear.

"Okay, so how do we respond?" the president asked.

Once again, the president showed his primary weakness, his inability to function as a commander and chief. Most of the time, he politicized an emergency; and when he couldn't do that, he would always come up wishy-washy and unable to make a decision. This was one of those times.

General Adams knew that the vice president would simply follow the president's lead. He also knew that Secretary Jameson would push for negotiations. Adams thought that Jameson was a smart man, but he was far too inexperienced for the job to which he was appointed. As soon as he finished this thought, Jameson voiced his opinion to call for negotiations. General Adams waited for him to finish, and then he interjected.

"We need to prepare a retaliatory attack on both the Chinese and the Russians and investigate the attack further," Adams said calmly. He saw the president's eyebrows drop with concern. Adams hated seeing this kind of weakness in the president.

"Give me an hour, and I will know if it was the Russians or the Chinese," Adams continued.

"Attacking either concerns me deeply—" the president began when an aide burst into the room. Every eye turned to her as she whispered to the secretary of state.

Hawaii

The torpedo launch was detected by the *USS John Finn* as it left the shallow waters near Iroquois Point on the southern shore of the island of Oahu, Hawaii. The *USS John Finn* was a newly commissioned destroyer that was preparing for a mission to the Persian Gulf. The operations specialist who detected the torpedo launch immediately communicated the event to the commander of the vessel. Everyone in the control room was alarmed and confused by the detection. The commander called for general quarters, and as soon as the communication went out, the explosion was felt by everyone aboard the vessel.

The blast of the two-megaton nuclear warhead created a large blast radius that engulfed the *USS John Finn*. Within seconds, there were a dozen hull breaches, and flames spread throughout the vessel. Everyone onboard the *USS John Finn* would soon perish by flame or water.

The initial blast created a vacuum that pulled water in from every direction and then violently spat it back out. This was the effect that the Russians were looking for when they developed the nuclear torpedo.

Ten miles away, the USGS observation station near Mount Tantalus detected an event registering 4.3 on the Richter scale. Almost simultaneously, they received tsunami warnings from almost every buoy on the southern shore.

Airman Howard Jacobs stood near the western end of the runway at Hickam Air Force Base, which was located along the southern shore of Oahu. He was repairing a landing light when he heard the explosion. He turned to face the sound and saw a huge mushroom cloud—which consisted of flame, smoke, and water—rise above the horizon. Never had he ever witnessed anything like that before. Within seconds, the ocean began to pull back away from the shore until all he could see was land where water once was.

"Holy…," Jacobs began.

Then he saw what looked like a growing cloud along the horizon. He stood there slack-jawed, watching until he saw what he recognized as a wave of water at least ninety feet tall.

He dropped the wrench that was in his hand and began to run. In his heart, he knew that running was futile, but he couldn't think of a reason to stop.

Valerie Bellows decided to spend the day on the beach. She wanted to practice surfing, but the waves just weren't right that day. So instead, she decided on sail boarding. She had a nice wind that pulled her along the shore near Iroquois Point. She was sailing west along the shore when she saw the explosion. It was several miles from shore, but she knew that it had to have been something big. A moment ago, she was in about fifteen feet of water; and within seconds of the explosion, her sailboard was lying on solid ground. She hopped off the board and looked around.

"Where did all the water go?"she asked herself in confusion.

A moment later, she realized what was happening. The tsunami wave grew in the distance, getting bigger and bigger. Valerie knew that she was about to die, and she closed her eyes and said a prayer.

"Lord Jesus, thank you for the life that you've given me. Thank you for my family and friends. Please, Lord, protect them from what is about to happen. In Jesus Christ's name, I pray. Amen," Valerie prayed aloud.

Valerie opened her eyes in time to see the wave as it slammed into her. At no point did she feel terror. She knew that she was about to meet Jesus, and for her, that was the most exciting thing that she could think of.

Washington, D.C.

Back in Washington, as the aide was speaking to the secretary of state, everyone in the room could see the horror in his eyes.

"What is it, Tyler?" the president asked.

"Uh…sir…it's Hawaii," he replied.

The secretary went on to explain the situation in Hawaii. By the time he was finished, they had local Hawaiian news up on the television. Eyewitnesses said that there had been a large explosion a few miles south of the island of Oahu. The explosion created a tsunami wave that, conservatively, was ninety feet tall. There was some video of the wave crashing into the shoreline.

The wave had swept over Hickam Air Force Base, which was a complete loss. As many as fifty aircraft were destroyed. The wave had crested only sixty feet from the beach and had come crashing down on the southern shore, with waters going all the way to Highway H-1 near the base of the mountains. The wave accelerated through the channel going into Pearl Harbor and decimated the Pacific Fleet that was stationed there. Apparently, the *USS John Finn* had been destroyed by the initial explosion. Thankfully, two United States attack submarines was patrolling north of the island and survived. They were in pursuit of four enemy submarines. Current speculation was that these submarines were from the North Korean Navy, but only time would tell.

The news of the attacks deflated the room. The president sat slumped in his seat while the Security Council members shouted out orders to their subordinates. America was at war with North Korea and possibly China or Russia, maybe both.

CHAPTER 68

Ford

Ford decided that he would ride a couple of miles on his stationary bike while he watched the financial news. At the opening bell, everything seemed pretty flat. Ford was surprised that the financial markets had not taken more of a hit after the terrorist attacks in New York City and Nashville.

He had been riding for about twenty minutes when a news anchor broke in with an important alert. Apparently, Honolulu had been hit by a tsunami, and most of the city was still underwater. The news anchor expected the water to subside over the next several hours. Shockingly, the United States Navy suffered huge losses as much of the Pacific Fleet was currently stationed at Pearl Harbor.

Honolulu had a population of almost four hundred thousand, and there was speculation that the death toll could be in the hundreds of thousands. Ford stopped pedaling and went to sit on the couch. He called Abby from the other room.

"Abby, something horrible has happened in Hawaii," Ford said sadly.

Abby and Ford watched the news broadcast in horror.

"A minute ago, they said that the number of dead could be in the hundreds of thousands," he continued.

Abby was silent, and Ford knew that she was praying for those affected. Ford said a quick prayer as well.

"How could this happen—" Ford was just asking when the news anchor said that there were eyewitnesses who saw an impossibly large mushroom cloud near the horizon south of the island.

"What?" Abby said in anguish. "Did he say mushroom cloud?"

"Yes, I think that is what he said," Ford replied.

Just then, something on the bottom of the screen caught Ford's eye. He noticed that the Dow Jones Industrial Average was down five hundred points, which was about 3 percent. He wondered if the disaster in Hawaii had an impact on the stock market. He didn't see how it could have an impact, but the market seemed so driven by speculation these days it was scary. He read a couple of years ago that rampant speculation was the reason for a large market crash several years ago, and because of that crash, they implemented a safety net that paused trading if the market was rising or falling too fast.

Ford sat with Abby and watched the news for a few more minutes when the anchor came back on. The anchor's mood was exasperated, and he was breathless. Ford had never witnessed a national news anchor showing so much emotion. The news anchor proceeded to announce what was disturbing him.

"Ladies and gentlemen," the anchor said with a pause. There was sadness in his voice. "Ladies and gentlemen," he repeated, "there has been another tsunami in another American city."

Ford wasn't sure if the anchor was being sincere or if he was simply trying to be more dramatic. The anchor paused and looked to his co-anchor, who looked just as horrified.

"The cities of San Francisco and Oakland have been devastated by another tsunami!" the anchor exclaimed. He paused and looked to his co-anchor, as if waiting for her to say something.

His co-anchor, who was visibly shaken, finally spoke up, "The tsunami originated about five miles west of San Francisco. There have been eyewitness accounts of a wall of water several hundred feet high." She paused. The co-anchor took a deep breath and finished, "Details are sparse, but it seems that a large barge carrying a full load of cargo was exiting the Golden Gate straits when the wave hit." She paused again. "Apparently, the wave picked up the huge barge and slammed it into the middle span of the Golden Gate Bridge," she ended with tears in her eyes.

The anchor continued with more details, "We are just getting pictures from our local affiliate helicopter." He looked confused and seemingly looked past the camera and then to his right.

"Apparently, we are having difficulty with the video coming from the local station—" he was starting to say when a video popped up on the screen for a few seconds.

"Oh my gosh!" Abby said with a shocked look on her face.

The image on the screen was of the Golden Gate Bridge ripped in half and falling into the bay. Tears ran down Abby's face as she looked at Ford in silence.

Ford didn't know what to say or do. He wondered what was happening. The image of the bridge was replaced by the anchor and co-anchor, both visibly distraught.

Out of nowhere, the co-anchor burst out, "Mom, please call me!"

Ford could totally understand her losing it if her mom lived in San Francisco.

"Mom, if you are okay, please contact me!" she added, now completely in tears.

The camera zoomed in on the anchor. He looked to his left for a moment to where his co-anchor was. Ford could tell that he was sad as well.

"It is unclear how much damage there is, but it seems that the tsunami covered 80 percent of the San Francisco area. Only the southernmost area of the bay, near San Jose, was left untouched," he read. "It looks like the wave had enough force to push deep into Oakland as well. Much of both San Francisco and Oakland are under the water." He seemed to be struggling. "The population of the San Francisco Bay area is slightly more than eight million people. It is impossible to know how many people have perished," he finished.

Ford thought to himself, *How many people have died today? One million, two million, more?* The thought was impossible. Ford couldn't stand to watch the news any longer, and he switched it off.

"Abby, will you go on a walk with me?" Ford asked.

Abby immediate nodded yes. Ford stood up and grabbed Abby's hand. They moved to the mudroom to get dressed for the weather.

CHAPTER 69

Samantha

It was Samantha's day off, and she was relaxing. It had been a stressful week with all that had happened in New York City, Nashville, and Paris. She sat down at her computer and started looking at the news. The first thing she saw was news that the Paris authorities were suggesting that the Eiffel Tower was most likely going to come down. They had attempted to shore up the damaged section, but too much damage had been done. Authorities said that a large crane was on its way to Paris. This crane would help disassemble the iconic tower. However, delivery of the crane wouldn't be for another three weeks, so authorities were concerned that the tower would fall before the crane could get there. Consequently, the surrounding area was cordoned off.

She flipped back to the home page of the popular news website and was taken aback by the dual news alerts of tsunamis in Hawaii and San Francisco, California. Both had sustained a tsunami wave of unfathomable size and devastation. It was estimated that millions had perished between both cities. The government had yet to reveal the cause of each tsunami, but already, eyewitness accounts from both locations said that a large explosion was seen on the horizon. A source at the USGS leaked that a seismic event had occurred in both locations, registering around 4.2 to 4.5

on the Richter scale. Another source said that if you combined the eyewitness accounts of the explosion and the seismic data, the only conclusion would be that a nuclear explosion detonated below the ocean's surface.

Sam wondered about the possibility of these tsunamis being caused by the detonation of two separate nuclear bombs. If these two tsunamis were the result of two nuclear detonations by enemy combatants, then that meant that the United States was not only engaged in a war with ISIS—it was at war with some other country or countries.

Sam sat there in complete disbelief, wondering who could have launched the nuclear weapons that caused so much destruction. Sam suspected that only Russia and China had the capability to launch this type of attack. Maybe North Korea, but no other enemy could possibly possess such weapons. If it were Russia or China, then an escalation could mean complete destruction of most of the world.

Sam stood up from her computer and decided that she was going to go to her storage room and see where she stood with their emergency supplies. She didn't have a lot of money to spend, but she knew that Rob would understand if she used a credit card to buy whatever supplies that she needed. She hoped that she had more time to get prepared for whatever was coming next.

CHAPTER 70

Washington, D. C.

General Adams had just heard back from his sources in the intelligence community and the Navy regarding the attack on the *USS George H.W. Bush* in the Mediterranean Sea. The consensus was that it was a Chinese submarine that had stealth capability. Based on that consensus, the general recommended an attack on the Chinese aircraft carrier *Shi Lang*. The United States had several assets in the area that could destroy the vessel.

England and France also supported a retaliatory strike, but the rest of the European Union wasn't sure. The NATO alliance seemed to be on the verge of collapse as most NATO countries didn't want to get involved in another war.

With regard to Honolulu and Pearl Harbor, there was public speculation that the North Koreans were involved, but the government did not substantiate any of those rumors. The rumors, of course, were true; and the *USS Ronald Reagan*, which was currently stationed in the East China Sea, had orders to retaliate with a two-megaton nuclear warhead on the western naval port at Haeju Bay and the eastern naval port of Ch'aho. It had been over seventy years since a nuclear weapon was detonated by the Americans in Japan, but this was hardly a first strike.

As weak as this president was, he had not hesitated to nuke North Korea. General Adams wondered how he would respond if the Security Council recommended a nuclear strike on Russia or China.

After some deliberation, the president called for a strike on the Chinese aircraft carrier in the Mediterranean Sea. Five minutes later, the Security Council witnessed the launch of six Tomahawk cruise missiles, each containing one thousand pounds of standard explosive munitions that would certainly destroy the *Shi Lang*. With the help of satellite video, they witnessed the impact of all six missiles. They hit with rapid succession, and the *Shi Lang* was broken in two before it finally sank below the surface of the ocean.

The president had placed a call to the Chinese leader seconds before the first Tomahawk hit its mark. The president explained that this was in retaliation for the attack on the *USS George H.W. Bush*. The Chinese leader adamantly denied the attack on the US aircraft carrier, but the president showed a brief display of strength and warned the Chinese leader that any additional retaliation would be answered by a factor of ten. Unfortunately, the world had seen this president declare similar warnings, and in the end, he never followed through. Hopefully, in this case, the president wasn't playing games.

While the exchange with China took place, another disaster was reported from San Francisco. The president immediately deployed FEMA and Homeland Security to both Honolulu and San Francisco. But with the San Francisco attack, the United States didn't have clear evidence of who the perpetrator was. It had the same signature as the Hawaii attack, but the Security Council highly doubted that

North Korea had the capability to reach the United States in a submarine.

"So either the Russians sold the nuke to North Korea, or China did," General Adams stated.

"Why would either make such a bold move?" the president questioned. "Both know that North Korea is a wild card."

"Right, but if the North Koreans were under orders by either Russia or China to only attack us, then it might make sense," Adams said. "But that means there is more coming."

The president was about to speak when they got word that the US military base at Baghdad had been hit, as did four other key locations in Syria. The primary suspect was a Russian destroyer in the Caspian Sea.

The president leaned back on his chair and rubbed his forehead with his left hand. He slid it down his nose to his chin and onto his lap. The last several years had aged this president, like it did so many others. It was arguably the most difficult job in the world.

"What the heck is going on here?" the president questioned. "Are you telling me that the Russians, the Chinese, and the North Koreans are all attacking us? All at the same stinking time?"

"So it seems," replied General Adams. Adams could see Secretary Jameson beginning to squirm. He definitely wasn't cut out to be secretary of state. "Sir, we need to retaliate against the Russian destroyer in the Caspian Sea," General Adams continued. "I have an asset in the Persian Gulf that can launch three Tomahawks in less than five minutes. I also recommend we hit another asset of theirs in the Mediterranean or in Syria."

"Which do you suggest?" the president asked.

Adams saw the president slump in his seat again. He found it disgusting that he so easily showed weakness. Adams looked around the room, and most everyone else held a similar stance.

"Sir, I recommend that we hit their two new military bases in Syria. The primary base near Damascus we can hit with B-2 bombers. That will give the Russians pause," Adams replied. "I think taking out the naval base in Tartus would serve two purposes: one, we take out some of the Russian Navy there; but two, we also take out some of the Syrian Navy. These two attacks will give us a strategic advantage if we have to execute additional strikes."

"Okay, do it!" the president ordered.

General Adams made the call. Within minutes, a dozen Tomahawk missiles were launched from a destroyer in the Mediterranean toward the naval port of Tartus. Again, a satellite feed showed the complete destruction of all Russian and Syrian vessels in the port. Additionally, it would be years before the port would be usable again.

The B-2 Stealth Bombers had launched and were en route. It would be a few minutes before they reached the launch coordinates. The satellite feed switched to the new Russian base. The Security Council received word that the munitions had been dropped. General Adams ordered a dozen 1500-pound bunker-buster gravity bombs to be dropped. Modern gravity bombs still had some remote navigational capability, and each bomb hit its target within ten feet. In minutes, the council witnessed the complete destruction of the Russian military base in Syria.

General Adams stood tall as he watched the carnage. He gave no outward sign of remorse. The president looked at him and wondered how he could feel nothing. But inside,

Adams felt a twinge of guilt for any civilian who had been caught in the crossfire.

A warship in the Persian Gulf launched six Tomahawk cruise missiles at the Russian destroyer in the Caspian Sea, and within minutes, the Security Council witnessed its complete destruction.

A moment later, the general received word that a ballistic nuclear submarine in the *USS Ronald Reagan's* carrier group was now ready to launch the two nukes on North Korea, and the general was waiting confirmation of the launch codes. The president, the secretary of state, and the general all entered the codes and executed the launch. In seconds, two ballistic nuclear missiles were on their way to their target. The first to detonate was the one set on Ch'aho on the east coast. Ch'aho was primarily a military facility, so very few civilian casualties would occur. The satellite feed went completely white as the bomb detonated. Soon a large cloud was seen covering the entire area. The base at Haeju was bigger and contained more civilians, but it was the price that North Korea had to pay. The number of lives lost in America would far exceed those lost in North Korea by more than a tenfold. The satellite video provided a similar scene in Haeju as it had in Ch'aho.

The room had become very quiet. The killing of several hundred thousand people could be sobering. Even General Adams felt the pain in his stomach.

The president placed a call to the North Korean leader, but he refused to talk. It seemed that things would only get worse. Fortunately, for the Americans, the North Koreans' military capabilities were lacking compared to those of the United States of America.

The president wasn't sure how much worse the day could get, and then he felt the first explosion.

CHAPTER 71

Christopher

After all the evidence was examined, the CIA found that Ed was indeed the mastermind behind the Paris attacks. There still was the question of this Mahdi person that Ed had mentioned. So far, no evidence could be found that provided the identity of this person, but it was clear that there was a person who had been funding Ed. The director ordered Chris and Sara home for briefing on their next assignment.

It had been several days since their moment in the catacombs, but neither Chris nor Sara said anything to the other about the kiss. Chris sat on the seat next to Sara on the 747 that was traveling to Washington, DC. Sara was staring out the window, watching the ocean thirty-six thousand feet below. The captain said that they would be landing in Ronald Reagan Washington National Airport in less than two hours. Sara had her long dark hair pulled back in a ponytail, and Chris spent the last few minutes admiring her small neck and delicate ears. He noted the slight curve at the end of her nose as she continued to look out the window. Her high cheekbones gave her a somewhat exotic appeal. Chris wondered where her ancestors had originated. He marveled at how her thin upper lip gently met with her thicker lower lip.

He kept remembering how soft those lips had felt against his. He couldn't figure out what she saw in him.

For God's sake, I'm fifteen years older than her, Chris thought to himself. *She could have anyone.*

"Take a picture!" Sara said to the window. "It will last longer." She turned to him with a smile.

Chris knew that his face must be a deep shade of red, but he didn't care.

"Hang on, let me get my camera." He laughed as he pretended to look for it. Sara playfully smacked his shoulder and laughed.

Chris hadn't ever heard such a lovely sound. To him, it was the laughter of an angel. That thought made him smile even more. His eyes met hers, and he was caught. There was nothing that he could do to escape her now. She gently touched his cheek with her hand and held it for a moment. He pressed into her hand slightly, soaking in every moment of her touch.

Chris couldn't stop smiling, but then he realized that he would need to say something, and his smile began to fade. Noticing that he was losing his smile, Sara cocked her head slightly, and her smile diminished as well.

"What?" Sara questioned.

Chris wasn't sure what to say and was trying to sort through his feelings. "Sorry, but I was just thinking, when we get to DC, we can't lead anyone to believe…," Chris started and then trailed off. "Uh, I mean, that if we are…," he tried to continue and paused.

Sara looked at him with a straight face, waiting for him to continue.

"I mean…are we? Ummm…," Chris stammered.

Sara held her stare for a few minutes, and then he saw something in her eyes. It was a glimmer, and soon her lips shared the joke. Her smile broadened, and he knew that she was playing with him.

"You're playing with me!" Chris exclaimed. "Aren't you?"

"Yes," Sara replied simply.

Chris had never been good with women and didn't know what she was saying.

"Yes," Sara repeated, "yes, I'm playing with you." She smiled. "And yes, we are."

Chris didn't say anything at first and then started to smile.

"So I get it. We need to act like we are partners and not lovers," Sara stated.

"Lovers?" Chris asked with a smile.

Sara flushed a bit and then laughed. "Well, if you play your cards right, maybe someday." She held his gaze for a moment longer and then began looking out the window again.

Chris couldn't stop smiling. Sara was so beautiful, and he just couldn't figure out what she could see in him. The last few weeks had been a roller-coaster ride of epic proportions. He hoped that during the next few days, they could relax a bit. Little did he know that minutes after they landed at Ronald Reagan, the White House went on lockdown.

CHAPTER 72

Ford

Ford and Abby came back inside after finishing their walk through the woods. Abby had become much better on snowshoes, and he only needed to help her up from the snow on a couple of occasions. Snowshoeing wasn't as easy as some people made it look. Ford had become fairly proficient over the last couple of years. He now felt comfortable on any hike in the woods, regardless of how deep the snow was.

Ford knocked the snow off their snowshoes and hung them up in the mudroom. He watched with admiration as Abby removed her jacket and snow pants. She was wearing a fleece sweatshirt, which clung to her form, and black yoga pants, which seemed to be the rage these days. Ford could appreciate the yoga pants on most women, but they were especially appealing on Abby.

A few years ago, as they closed in on forty, both Abby and Ford began to take better care of themselves. They exercised almost daily and ate far healthier than they ever had. Moving to the lodge had helped them achieve this as well. Growing their own food and tending to animals ensured that they didn't have a lot of time to sit around. Being miles from civilization also made it less convenient to pick up fast food. Abby had done well to keep her form through the years. Sure, she had put on a couple of pounds since they got married, but living in the country kept her fit. Abby was hanging up her jacket and had her back to Ford. He smiled and moved up behind her. He slid his arms around her waist and moved in closer. She instinctively wrapped her hands around his and pressed back onto him. She tipped her head back as he nuzzled into her neck. He breathed in the scent of the shampoo that she had used earlier washing her hair. He caught a slight smell of the coconut butter lotion that she used as well. His lips brushed against her neck as he moved his mouth closer to her ear. In this moment, he could not have been happier. With everything else going on in the world, he was home, with Abby, the love of his life.

"I love you, Abby!" he whispered.

He felt her press in closer before turning to meet him. She looked up at him slightly with a smile that made Ford feel completely loved. Her light-brown eyes shared the smile as they stared at each other.

"Ford, you are the love of my life," Abby said. "I don't know what I would do without you."

Ford knew that Abby loved him, but he always was amazed how those words made him feel. He kissed her softly, and then they held each other for a few moments before they had to get back to the real world.

Ford went to his office to check his e-mail. When he sat down, he noticed that a web browser he had left open to the financial pages updated the stock market numbers. He refreshed the page, thinking that maybe there was an error, but there wasn't an error. The Dow Jones Industrial Average had dropped over two thousand points since the market opened only three hours earlier. That was about a 12 percent drop already. He clicked on the headline "Unprecedented

Crash!" and brought up the current story on the market. There was talk about the market safety nets not seeming to work. The current drop was far beyond the threshold for signaling a pause in the markets. There was some speculation that the change happened so quickly that it blew through the barrier. Immediately, Ford dismissed that idea. He knew enough about computers to know that that didn't make sense.

So far, no one theorized that it could have been the result of a hack into the stock market computer systems, but that was the first thing that Ford considered. Ford figured if he was thinking about it, then surely someone of importance was also thinking about it. The political-correctness culture that dominated politics had spread like a malignant cancer into every aspect of life. An entire generation had grown up being too afraid to hurt anyone's feelings. Sure, there was a time where restraint was a good idea, but like most things, political correctness was best served in moderation.

Ford wasn't sure how the state of the stock market related to everything else that was going on around the world, but he knew that a crash right now couldn't have been more devastating to the country and possibly the world. Ford decided that he needed to get back to work on his end-times research.

Ford began to create a timeline of end-times events. He had never attempted to assign dates to these events because Jesus was quite clear in the book of Matthew that only God knows the hour and the day of His second coming. Matthew 24:36 says, "No one knows about that day or hour, not even the angels in heaven, nor the Son, but only the Father." Ford realized that God wanted his children to watch for the signs that will signal the second coming of Jesus. He also discovered that there was order and that these events could be placed along a timeline to show their relative position.

A few months before, he had purchased a large whiteboard and hung it in his office. On the whiteboard, he drew a timeline. The Bible spoke of seven seals that would be opened in the time of the end. These seals were discussed in the book of Revelation chapter 6. The first event on the timeline to the far left was the "reestablishment of Israel as a nation." This event was chronicled in Ezekiel 36 and 37, and it was important because all end-times events were dependent on it.

The second event was the opening of the first seal, which represented the rider on a white horse bent on conquest. Ford continued to struggle with the meaning of this horseman. Most commentaries thought this rider represented the Antichrist coming into the scene. Not that he would be in control but that he would begin his silent rise within the world of global politics. Ford also thought that it had potential ties to the rise of Antichrist behavior and false teachers. Clearly, the world was inundated with false teachers and Antichrist behavior. Lastly, there was a tie to the fall of Babylon (the modern nation of Iraq). With the help of other modern commentators, Ford found a link between the "head of gold" in Daniel 2, the "beast that resembled a lion" in Daniel 7, and now the "rider on the white horse" found in the book of Revelation. Coincidently, prior to his removal from Iraq, Saddam Hussein had commissioned many paintings and murals of himself on a white horse to be displayed throughout the country.

There was little doubt in Ford's mind that the prophecy regarding the first seal and the fall of Iraq had already come to pass. It was also clear to Ford that this was only the beginning of the birth pains. The next event on the timeline was the opening of the second seal, which was represented by a rider on a red horse, who would take peace from the world. Ford believed there was a tie between the "chest and arms of silver" in Daniel 2, "the beast that resembled a bear" in Daniel 7, the "Persian ram" in Daniel 8, and now the "rider on a red horse" found in the book of Revelation. Everything associated with this event pointed toward Persia (the modern nation of Iran). Ford strongly believed that Iran was on the verge of rushing out to the west, north, and south, as the prophecy in Daniel 8:4 suggested would happen.

Ford had been following the news for years in search of events that might be the fulfillment of prophecy or at least give a clue to the coming fulfillment of prophecy. He knew that Iran was already in control of Iraq, except for the area controlled by ISIS. Iran had a strong presence in Yemen to the south and Lebanon and Syria to the west. In Daniel 8, the ram rushed out from Susa, which is located in the southwestern portion of Iran near the border with Iraq. Rushing north could mean to parts of Iraq or Turkey. With all the turmoil in the Middle East and the increased presence of Turkish troops in Iraq, it made sense to Ford that Iran might possibly move against Turkey. Russia also was to the north, but Ford found it difficult to believe that Iran would consider an invasion of Russia.

The concept of the Persian ram rushing out to conquer the Middle East seemed incredible to Ford because in order for Iran to conquer the Middle East, it would have to attack Turkey and Saudi Arabia, among other Sunni nations. What an amazing feat this would be to accomplish.

This led Ford down another path of thought. The population of Iran almost entirely practiced the Shiite (also called Shia) version of Islam. The majority of the remaining Islamic world practiced the Sunni version of Islam. Ford grabbed a book from the shelf behind him. He wanted to confirm a suspicion.

"There it is!" Ford exclaimed aloud to himself.

He was reading about the differences between Sunnis and Shiites. It all came down to their belief regarding who was supposed to be the leader of the Islamic world. This leader would be in control of the Islamic caliphate. This leader would have the title caliph and would be the political, military, and religious leader of the entire Muslim world. The disagreement regarding who would be this leader began right after Muhammad died in the seventh century. The Sunnis believed that the next leader should be the one voted on based on a consensus of the Islamic communities. The Shiites believed that only a person from Muhammad's bloodline can be the leader.

From the moment of Muhammad's death, the Islamic world had been divided. This provided further evidence that the revived Islamic caliphate was represented by the "feet and toes of iron and clay" in Daniel 2. Iron and clay don't mix, nor do Sunni and Shia Islam. It also provided more evidence as to why Iran would consider attacking the rest of the Islamic world.

There was another name that Ford had read about recently. He thumbed through the book that was in his hand until he found the page that he was looking for. The name he found was *Mahdi*. This Mahdi was prophesied to be the Islamic messiah who would come to lead the Muslim world. In other words, when the Mahdi returned, he would become the caliph of the revived Islamic caliphate.

The pieces started falling into place for Ford. So if the revived Islamic caliphate was the Antichrist Empire from which the Antichrist would rule, and the Mahdi was prophesized to come and rule the Islamic caliphate, there was a clear connection that the Mahdi was the Antichrist.

"Wow!" Ford exclaimed. "The Mahdi is the Antichrist!"

Ford had always wondered about the history between Islam and Christianity. It had been a violent history from the beginning, and it seemed that it might be violent until the end.

CHAPTER 73

Samantha

Sam had just returned from the store with additional supplies that she thought would be needed if there was an emergency. She flipped on the television so that she could listen to more of the coverage on the tsunamis while she put away the groceries. From the other room, she heard more disturbing news.

"This just in," the news anchor announced calmly. "There are unsubstantiated accounts of two nuclear explosions within the borders of North Korea."

Sam could tell that the anchor was having difficulty believing such news. Sam found it hard to believe as well, and she also found it irresponsible for the news station to report that it was nuclear bombs without more information. Spreading false rumors like that could start a panic.

"Our sources in the USGS picked up two separate seismic events with readings ranging from 3.5 to 4.7 on the Richter scale," the anchor reported. "One source reported seeing a large plume of smoke north of Seoul, Korea, but no news has come from government sources to substantiate the report. Jack Trip is live in Seoul," the anchor said. "Hey, Jack, what are you hearing?" The video was rough and a little distorted.

"Well, Brad, there have been several eyewitnesses who say they heard a distant explosion and saw smoke in the distance," Jack reported. "Most accounts say that the smoke was seen northwest of Seoul."

"Is there any word from the local authorities?"Brad asked.

"No, so far, the police have been quiet," Jack answered, "which is odd for the local police here."

Sam continued to watch for a few minutes and then went back to unpacking the groceries. She wondered about the news out of Korea. When she was done with the groceries, she decided she would spend a little time working out her thoughts on the war that was described in Ezekiel 38–39.

Sam had come close to finding some answers about a week earlier. She had been distracted by earthquakes and tsunamis ever since. She was working on the word *rosh* and wanted to know if it could be pointing toward Russia. There was evidence that the word *rosh* was probably a noun, but there wasn't sufficient evidence to call it a proper noun. The common translation was "chief," so as a noun, it was used to identify a *chief.* There seemed to be evidence that there were people who lived during Ezekiel's time who could have been identified by the name *Rosh*, but there was no evidence that those people lived in Russia. Almost all accounts pointed to Asia Minor, specifically Turkey.

Sam could only conclude that the proper interpretation of Ezekiel 38:3 is "Set your face toward Gog, of the land of Magog, the prince, chief of Meshech and Tubal" rather than, "Set your face toward Gog, of the land of Magog, the prince of Rosh, Meshech and Tubal."

Sam smiled at her apparent breakthrough, but then she frowned because she may have just helped Ford's case.

"Dang it!" Sam exclaimed, but she smiled despite herself.

CHAPTER 74

Washington, D. C.

"Did you feel that?" the president asked.

An instant later, the door to the Situation Room flew open, and the head of the president's Secret Service detail came charging in. General Adams shook his head, remembering when entrance to the Situation Room was prohibited by anyone except the Security Council, but this president had thrown tradition out the window and allowed almost anyone to barge in. Already, they had been interrupted twice by White House aides. Who knew what these people had clearance for?

"Excuse me, sir," the Secret Service man addressed the president, "but we've had a breach of the White House perimeter, and we need to get to the bunker."

Outside the Situation Room, there was a detail of Secret Service along with a few marines. The president and the members of the Security Council were being ushered down the hall when they felt the second explosion. The procession continued to move down the hall toward the elevators that would take them to the bunker.

"What is going on out there?" the president demanded.

"Sir, we are not entirely sure, but at least one vehicle has rammed the northwest gate," the Service man replied.

"But that was more than a gate being rammed," the president said.

They had just reached the elevator, and everyone began to climb in.

"Yes, sir, the vehicle seems to have been rigged with explosives," the Service man answered. The doors of the elevator closed, and they began to make their descent.

"I want full video when we get into the bunker," the President announced.

"Yes, sir!" the Service man replied.

A moment later, the door of the elevator opened to the bunker, and the Security Council filed out. The council took their place at the large oval table in the bunker command center. A dozen Secret Service agents were placed at the bottom of the elevator, as well as at the top.

The closed-caption surveillance system was engaged, and everyone began to get an idea of what was happening outside. There were two dozen cameras that could be viewed on the big screen, but right now, the northwest gate was the main event. As far as they could tell, the gate had been completely breached by a second vehicle. The vehicles appeared to be cargo vans. The first van lay on its side near the front gate. It lay there like a burnt-out carcass. The second van had obviously breached the gate when it detonated, and it lay beside the guard shack.

Other cameras showed dozens of military personnel in positions, attempting to defend America's most famous residence. The president was thankful that the first family was currently at Camp David. As he was thinking about his family, he noticed something flying above the north lawn on one of the video displays. To him, it looked like a mini-drone that an amateur enthusiast would fly.

"What is that?" the president asked, pointing to camera 12.

Assuming that the president wanted that view on the big screen, the operator switched the view. In that moment, everyone knew what they were.

"Sir, that seems to be an aerial drone," an operator replied. "Control currently has identified twelve drones within the perimeter of the White House."

Camera 12 flashed all white, and when it cleared, everyone could see that the entire viewable area was on fire. Three more cameras flashed and then showed the resulting fire. Whoever was operating the drones first took out the snipers on the roof. It looked like maybe one drone was taken out before it had delivered its payload.

External cameras showed that more than 50 percent of the rooftop was currently on fire. Additionally, military personnel began filing out onto the roof. It seemed that their primary targets were the drones. With four drones detonated and one taken out, it seemed that seven more were in play. As everyone was watching this play out, a third van drove through the area that was once the northwest gate. More than twenty military personnel attempted to hold their ground, but the van's momentum brought it to the base of the White House, where it exploded in a flash.

Ten stories below the surface, those in the bunker couldn't feel the blast, but based on the video, it must have been huge. The canopy that covered the north door was partially destroyed and was on the verge of collapse.

"Holy crap!" the secretary of state, Tyler Jameson, exclaimed. "Look, one of those drones is in the vestibule." Everyone watched in disbelief as they saw it hover and move toward the stairs. Shots were fired at the drone, but it wasn't taken out. It finally made its way to the second floor when it detonated. The central hall was engulfed in flames, and several interior walls were blown out by the explosion. In seconds, much of the second floor was burning out of control.

The president watched in disbelief as his world was consumed by fire. He slumped down on his chair unnoticed. He sat there with his head in his hands and thought about his family. He picked up the phone and dialed Camp David.

General Adams heard part of the conversation between the president and his wife. In the general's mind, of all the phone calls that needed to be made, the one that the president was currently on was the least important. When the president finally hung up the phone, General Adams spoke up.

"Sir, we have troops from the Washington Police Department, the National Guard, and the Marines on their way," Adams announced. "Honestly, we don't know what we are up against right now, and we have no idea what they want."

Jared and the other five members of his team were on the tour of the US Capitol building when the alarm sounded. His team had planned for this day carefully so that they could ensure the largest number of casualties. The tour had just begun, and fortunately, they were within twenty feet of the primary entry to the rotunda. The rotunda was where the legislative branch of the government held their votes. At that moment, ironically, the Senate was voting on a bill to provide additional funding for the war on terror.

When the alarm went off, there was a flurry of activity. Security officers would soon be on their way. As the tour guide was trying to corral all the tourists, Jared and his team made their move. It was unfortunate that the sergeant at arms already sealed the primary entrance to the rotunda, but Jared and his team had that covered. He signaled to one member, who immediately rushed the door and detonated his vest as the rest of the team moved to cover. The blast tore open the door and took out all security personnel in the area.

Now it is time to make a real change! Jared thought to himself. "Go!" he yelled to his team.

He and the four other members rushed into the room and spread out. The first two headed to opposite ends of the rotunda, where the House of Representatives and Senate filed in respectively. Another rushed to the far door to the library, and the fourth held his position at the front door. There was mass hysteria in the room, and only when Jared reached the main podium and threatened the majority Senate leader did they all quiet down.

"Okay, you jackals!" Jared yelled into the podium's microphone. "Everyone, sit down and shut up!" He did not intend to get so worked up, but the heat of the moment got to him. He took a breath to calm himself. "Here is what we're going to do," he spoke more calmly. He was feeling better about the way he was presenting himself now. "We only have a few moments before the stuff is going to hit the fan, so be quiet and listen to my instructions."

"We don't negotiate with terrorists," yelled the senator from Arizona.

Jared shook his head and pulled out a pistol that he just had printed this afternoon. It was incredible, the number of mechanical devices that could be created via 3-D printers these days. This device was made up of a composite of plastic and ceramic and was capable of firing up to three rounds before becoming nonfunctional.

Jared aimed the gun at the senator and slowly walked toward him. When he got within ten feet, he fired a ceramic bullet into the skull of the legislator. A gasp rose from the crowd as the man's head exploded, and he fell to the ground in a pile.

"Anyone else?" Jared screamed. He had lost his control again. He turned from his hostages and slowly walked back up to the podium. He knew that he had about twenty seconds before the security force arrived.

"I just wanted to say one more thing." Jared said.

"When in the course of human events it becomes necessary for one people to dissolve the political bands which have connected them with another and to assume among the powers of the earth, the separate and equal station to which the Laws of Nature and of Nature's God entitle them, a decent respect to the opinions of mankind requires that they should declare the causes which impel them to the separation.

We hold these truths to be self-evident, that all men are created equal, that they are endowed by their Creator with certain unalienable Rights, that among these are Life, Liberty and the pursuit of Happiness. That to secure these rights, Governments are instituted among Men, deriving their just powers from the consent of the governed."

Jared took a breath and continued to recite the Declaration of Independence,

"That whenever any Form of Government becomes destructive of these ends, it is the Right of the People to alter or to abolish it, and to institute new Government, laying its foundation on such principles and organizing its powers in such form, as to them shall seem most likely to effect their

Safety and Happiness. Prudence, indeed, will dictate that Governments long established should not be changed for light and transient causes; and accordingly all experience hath shewn that mankind are more disposed to suffer, while evils are sufferable than to right themselves by abolishing the forms to which they are accustomed. But when a long train of abuses and usurpations, pursuing invariably the same Object evinces a design to reduce them under absolute Despotism, it is their right, it is their duty, to throw off such Government, and to provide new Guards for their future security. Such has been the patient sufferance of these Colonies; and such is now the necessity which constrains them to alter their former Systems of Government," he finished.

Jared was amazed that he'd been able to get through his entire speech. He smiled a crooked smile and said, "It is time to free our country from the cancer that has become this government!"

With that, each member of his team detonated their vest, leaving the United States with only half of its legislative body.

CHAPTER 75

Nigel

The scene at the White House looked like something out of a movie, and Nigel and his team only had a few more minutes before the National Guard would arrive. Nigel's drone operator was the one to breach the White House and set the interior on fire. That drone was his last active drone, and he signaled to Nigel that he was ready to get out of there. Line of sight was helpful, but not necessary, to operate the drones. They were parked north of the White House, near the corner of I Street NW and Connecticut Avenue NW, to give them just enough of a view of the building. Nigel hoped that a perimeter had not already been setup as he shifted the van into drive and merged into traffic. He crossed I Street and headed north on Seventeenth Street and whispered, "Allahu Akbar," to himself.

Nigel heard sirens all around him; and when he passed M Street, a Washington, DC, Police Department cruiser pulled into the intersection behind him and stopped. He nervously watched the rearview mirror to make sure that he wasn't followed and continued to drive away toward freedom.

The plan was for the team to meet at the compound in Detroit and lie low for a few days. Ali said that he had another glorious job for him. Nigel was still in disbelief at how effective their attack was. He didn't know how many casualties there were, but he knew that they had struck terror into the hearts of the American people.

Nigel had been driving for several hours and needed to stop for gas. They avoided all toll roads to avoid as many traffic surveillance cameras as possible. He had just switched from I-70 to I-77 near Cambridge, Ohio, and noticed a sign for gas. Cambridge looked like a small town, and he hoped that they could get fuel and food and move on.

His drone operator had a Middle Eastern look and didn't speak very good English, so they agreed that he should stay in the van and lie low while Nigel pumped gas and picked up some burgers from the Wendy's that was attached to the gas station.

As Nigel pumped the gas, he imagined that Cambridge was a normal rural town full of white hicks who spent their days chewing tobacco and shooting squirrels. A moment later, two local boys drove up to the pump next to him. They were driving a jacked-up 4×4 truck with large tires and mud all over. He smiled to himself and continued pumping gas. When he was finished pumping gas, he took a look inside the van to make sure his partner was still at the back and then went into the store to pay. Of course, they would only pay with cash so as to not create a money trail.

After paying for his gas, he went to the other side of the store and got in line at Wendy's. The two local boys came in behind him, talking about the terrorist attacks that had occurred earlier that day.

"Man, I'm not a big fan of our government either, but someone has to do something about those rag heads," the taller one said.

"We need a president who isn't such a wuss and who will close the border," the other responded. "We have enough illegals here already."

"I don't know why they don't just kick them all out," the tall one said.

"Yeah, send them home, and then we can nuke the crap out of them," the other added. "Let's turn that desert into glass!"

"I wonder how long it will be before bozo declares martial law?" the tall one questioned.

Nigel hadn't thought about that. If they inflicted too much damage on the government, the president would eventually declare martial law. He wondered what that would mean to their ongoing operations. He imagined that the government would institute curfews and possibly try to confiscate weapons. As if reading his mind, the tall one shared his feelings on weapon confiscations.

"I tell you what!" the tall one started. "There is no way they are going to come and take my guns. They'll have to pry them from my cold, dead hands!" he added in a raised voice, which surely everyone in the store could hear.

Nigel placed his order and listened to the two rednecks continue to on about the government and the alien invasion. He wondered how many Americans shared their feelings. Nigel didn't really stay current with American politics, but he knew that most politicians were either too afraid to address the problem of illegal immigration or didn't want to. One thing was clear, though, and that was that the United States government was seriously broken.

CHAPTER 76

Copenhagen

By the end of day, in the United States, the Dow Jones Industrial Average had dropped almost 3,500 points for almost a 20 percent loss in value. The other exchanges didn't fare any better. The financial news found it odd that the safety nets weren't triggered to stop the free fall. However, Frederick was surprised that the market didn't lose more value during the slide.

The Asian markets were set to open in fifteen minutes, and futures were looking to start trading at over a 4 percent loss right off the bat. Based on the news cycle in Beijing and Tokyo, Frederick expected losses to follow close behind the American markets. News out of Europe didn't look much better.

"With any luck, the spiral will run out of control before they find the viruses," Frederick said. No one else was in the room, but he had become accustomed to talking to himself. Often he would actually hold short conversations with himself. On occasion, he would listen to himself talking to himself and wonder if he was going crazy, but then he would continue with the conversation anyway.

"I think the Asians will find it first," he told himself. "And the Europeans will be last. This should be pretty fun." He laughed.

"Dude, you're going totally crazy!" he exclaimed, again to himself.

"Yeah, I know," he replied. "We're friggin' nuts!" He laughed again. This time, he laughed so hard that he had trouble stopping; and by the time he was done, his stomach hurt so bad that it felt like he'd been punched in the gut by one of those MMA fighters.

Thankfully, the phone rang, and he was able to calm himself before picking it up. "Hello," Frederick answered.

"Are you set to go?" the caller asked.

"I need a few more days to get the malware ready," Frederick replied. "Once the malware is ready, we'll need to hack their network and drop it in. The virus is a modification of the one that I wrote for their stock market."

"Okay, get it done," the caller said. "I want to be ready very soon."

"Okay, okay," Frederick replied. With that, the caller hung up.

"Take your Allah and go bite me!" Frederick said to the phone.

Frederick had been working for Ali Basharat for over a year. He couldn't complain about the money, but Frederick felt underappreciated. Ali didn't care how things were done; he just wanted them done. He didn't recognize that building a virus was an art and not a science.

"I'm like Michelangelo, and you don't appreciate my Sistine Chapel!" Frederick shouted. "We've given you access to any computer system in the world, and do we get a thank-you?" Frederick asked the wall.

"Nooooo!" he answered. "Look at these hands! These are the hands of an artist!" he shouted louder.

Frederick began having more and more bouts with anger and had become increasingly violent.

"Why can't you just give me a friggin' thank-you!" he screamed into the room. With that, he abruptly jumped up from his desk chair, knocking it over in the process. He picked up his partially filled ceramic coffee cup and threw it against the far wall, leaving a trail of liquid across the floor.

His anger was getting the best of him, and he felt that he was losing control. He extended his arms over his head, stretched his whole body in the process, and finally brought his hands down upon his head and into his hair. His hands entangled with hair, he began to pull his fists. The pain was incredible, and finally he released his grasp, just short of ripping out his hair. The pain felt strangely good, and he decided that he was done working for the day.

"Screw you, Ali. And screw you, Allah!" he exclaimed. "I'm going out and getting myself drunk!"

Frederick had become more accustomed to cursing Allah. Frederick didn't believe in religion. He only believed in himself. He attempted to calm down by telling himself that he only had a few more days left before he could get out of this crappy apartment and get back to his home in Geneva, but those words only went so far. Tonight he would drink, and later he would find someone to take out his frustrations on. There was a small part of him that said he needed to stop hurting people. It was the other part, the one that liked hurting people that had begun to gain control. He wasn't sure if he could stop with simply hurting someone. He might have to do more.

CHAPTER 77

Ford

I t had been a couple days since the attacks on Washington. The country was reeling from everything that had happened. A large portion of the White House had burned to the ground. In those attacks, dozens of Secret Service personnel lost their lives, as well as many National Guard members. There were three vans rigged with explosives that breached the White House. A fourth van was stopped at Pennsylvania Avenue by a lone FBI agent. The news broadcast said that he was coming out of the Department of Treasury building when the first van exploded. According to reports, he heroically ran down Pennsylvania Avenue toward the first explosion. As he ran, he witnessed the second explosion at the gate and the third under the White House canopy. By the time he arrived at the northwest gate, the fourth van came barreling down the road toward him. The report said that he drew his weapon and emptied the magazine of his .45-caliber Glock 36 into the windshield of the van. A few of these shots hit their mark and took out the driver, which resulted in the van veering to the right and into the guard shack. The driver was killed by the gunfire, and the passenger was apprehended.

The news also reported that two other vans parked around the perimeter of the White House had been discovered. From these vans, the terrorists were able to operate unmanned drones that were used to attack security personnel. One of those drones actually made it into the White House and detonated. The Secret Service believed that it was this drone that caused the fire inside the White House.

Three of the terrorists found in the two vans had been captured. A fourth terrorist had run into a crowded restaurant to escape police and then detonated an explosive vest. According to the authorities, this explosion resulted in almost thirty fatalities.

Ford continued to watch the news with bewilderment. He and Abby had always felt safe, but the attacks in Washington, DC, changed that forever. ISIS claimed responsibility for the attacks. The FBI and CIA were working to determine if their claim was justified. Regardless, Ford knew that many Muslims in the United States would be the butt of much harassment in the coming days. When people fear something, they tend to attack it.

Ford and Abby decided that they would have John stay home from school that week and talked Tom into staying around the house as well. With everything that was going on, they just didn't think that it was a good idea to be in public. The nation's threat level had been set to its highest level. Some cities—like Chicago, Detroit, and New York— had established curfews. The National Guard, for almost thirty states, was placed in a ready status but were not yet deployed.

Ford had been to town the previous day and witnessed several men and women exercising their right to openly carry their firearms. They lived near a smaller town, and it was well-known that there were more guns than people in town. He really hoped that people didn't get out of control. Ford wondered what it was like for Muslims in larger cities.

The news got worse. The majority of the US senators were killed when multiple assailants detonated explosive vests within the US Capitol building during a critical vote on war finances. It was unclear how the government would function with over half of the legislative body dead. There were a dozen or so senators who had not been present for the vote, but it left most of the country without representation.

Earlier that day, the president had addressed the nation on television from an undisclosed location. He said that in light of the horrific tragedy at the capitol building, the government would continue functioning. He said that, given the unusual circumstances of the attack, they didn't have a plan on how they would proceed in Congress for the short term. He did say that they would schedule a national election to be held within three to six months so that they could fill all the open seats in the United States Senate.

The news continued to get worse. The US stock market had crashed on the first day that trading continued. It had gone down almost 20 percent. The Asian markets followed with an 18 percent loss. The European markets fared a little better with a 12 percent loss, but the following day, the US market dropped another 12 percent. The Asian markets had lost another 15 percent. The Europeans fared the worst on the second day with another drop of 23 percent. The US stock market decided that it would close the following day, and the Asian and European markets followed suit. Analysts weren't sure that the markets would fare any better when they opened again. Oil prices had only increased slightly to around $45, but gold and silver prices had increased by 23 percent and 35 percent respectively.

Ford had trouble digesting everything that he saw and read. There was just too much going on in the world. The speculation that North Korea had been nuked was confirmed by the president. The president said that North Korea was responsible for the tsunamis in Honolulu and San Francisco. He also confirmed reports of several attacks by Russia against the United States' military assets in Iraq and Syria and the resulting retaliatory strikes against Russia in the Middle East. The president said that he was in contact with the Russian president and felt confident that the attacks would not escalate. He confirmed that the Chinese had attacked an aircraft carrier in the Mediterranean Sea. The aircraft carrier was damaged but would soon be repaired. In retaliation, the United States sank a Chinese aircraft carrier in the Mediterranean Sea. Tensions were high throughout the world.

With all the craziness going on in the world, Ford decided that he would check in with Samantha and Zack. Ford sat down at his desk and switched on his computer. While he waited for it to start up, he looked out the window. The scene outside was so calming. The snow was falling, and everything looked fresh and new. At a glance, life could have been perfect, but he knew that beyond the view of this window, chaos was about to erupt.

CHAPTER 78

Zack

I t had been a few days since Zack looked at the news. He was working around the house, getting things prepared. The last few nights, he had been having more dreams. He dreamed of Ford and Samantha. In one dream, he saw Ford leading a group of people to some unknown destination. There were dozens of people following him in the wild. In another dream, Samantha was gathering people to herself. It seemed that with the chaos going on in the world, more and more people expressed interest in Samantha's faith. He saw Samantha in a river dunking people in a ceremony that might have been a baptism.

Zack was not accustomed to having dreams that were so vivid. After he finished stacking the wood that he split in the morning, he decided that he should check out his e-mail. He turned on his computer and then went into the living room to build a fire in the woodstove. The cold had really started to get to him. It was like it soaked into his bones, and he couldn't shake off the cold. He decided that he would sweat it out. He got a fire going and built it up so that, within a half hour or so, he wouldn't be able to sit in the room wearing anything more than a pair of shorts. He didn't like getting old.

When he got back to his computer, there was a notification that he had e-mail, but first he wanted to check the news.

On most days, Zack didn't want to know what was going on in the world. He was satisfied to simply live out his life in the woods, but after reading the news for about an hour, he had mixed emotions. The incredible news out of Washington, DC, was disturbing. He had never been a big fan of the government, but the terrorists had created a situation that could easily change to anarchy at a moment's notice. Zack couldn't believe that the president hadn't already declared martial law, but Zack was thankful that he didn't. Zack decided that he would go into town and pick up some more ammunition later in the day.

However, the most disturbing news for Zack was the news out of Honolulu and San Francisco. Zack couldn't believe that his second dream had come true as well. The death toll in the two disasters was over a million people. The sheer number of deaths was unimaginable.

Finally, Zack decided to open his e-mail. The first message that he noticed was the one from Ford.

Hey Zack,

I hope you are well, my friend. I have to tell you, I'm concerned about everything that is going on in our country. I wonder how long until they declare martial law. We have prepared for almost any emergency here at the lodge, but I do wish that I had more people here to help in case things get out of control. I know that you are all set there, but I wish that you were here, my brother! Your dreams continue to freak me out. I'm really scared about the third dream. I keep hearing people say that if we lose power, we'll be sent back into the 1800s, but I think it will be more like the 1100s. In the 1800s, people were used to living without power and, for the most part, were self-sufficient. Without power, the highly dependent people in this country won't last long. Millions would die in the chaos that follows. Grocery stores will be emptied in days without any hope of them being refilled. Then all the needy will strike out at those who have prepared. I don't really feel prepared to repel all the potential attacks. I know you are aware of all this stuff. I just need to vent.

I hope that you are safe. Let me know if you have any more dreams.

Take care,

Ford

Zack understood where Ford was coming from. Zack knew all too well that without others to help, he was prime for getting picked off. He decided that he would invite both Ford and Samantha, and their families, to join him. He wondered how much time they had.

CHAPTER 79

Samantha

The past few days had been busy for Samantha and her family. Rob had taken a couple of days off, and the boys were home because the school stayed closed due to the terrorist attacks. The whole country seemed like it was trying to recover from the events of the last few weeks.

Sam's family took the opportunity to finish their preparation for an emergency and to discuss what was going on in the world. Jacob outwardly seemed unaffected by the events that had transpired, but Sam asked Rob to talk to him anyway. In the last few months, Rob and Jacob had become closer, and she thought that if Jacob had any concerns, he might share them with Rob.

Isaac, on the other hand, was more emotional and had expressed his fears about the state of the world. Sam and Rob told them that they were prepared for almost any emergency and that they needed to pray for peace every day. One thing that Isaac said struck Sam as important. He had expressed concern that they didn't have any firearms in the house to protect them from bandits. Sam had smiled at the word *bandit*, but then in retrospect, she knew that he was right.

Later that night, after the boys had gone to bed, Rob and Sam sat in the living room talking about everything.

"I know that we have always said that we didn't want guns in the house, but I think it is time to reevaluate that stance," Sam said.

"I've been thinking about that all day since our talk with Isaac," Rob started, "and I think that he's right."

They both sat in silence for a moment. It was difficult to foresee what the future would bring, but right now, they would be unable to protect themselves if confronted by criminals.

"I think that we need to consider purchasing a shotgun, as well as a handgun," Rob said. "But I also want all four of us to go to a class on gun safety."

"I agree completely, but I think we should also buy a .22," Sam replied. "And maybe a handgun for both of us."

Rob nodded in agreement. It might seem weird to buy so many guns in such a short time, but right now wasn't a time to react slowly.

"It is going to be expensive to purchase these guns and a fair amount of ammunition," Rob started. "We'll have to dip into our savings to do it."

"I know, but this seems like a worthy purpose for the money," Sam replied.

They decided that the next day, they would go to the sporting goods store in town and look at some guns. After they were done talking about guns and emergency supplies, Sam started thinking about Brian. She hadn't heard from him in a few days and wondered how he was doing. It was late, but she decided that she would send him a text.

"Hey, Brian, are you okay?" Sam sent her message. She sat there for a while, thinking about everything that had happened. Just a month ago or so, the world had been a completely different place. Sure the world was far from perfect, but at least it didn't seem like it was on the edge of World War III.

"Yeah, Sam, I'm good. You?" Brian replied a few moments later.

"I was just thinking about this terrorist stuff and wondered about you. Wanted to make sure you're okay," Sam texted.

"It's crazy!" Brian replied. "Crazy! I feel like I need a vacation."

"Yeah, but a vacation seems pretty far-fetched right now. :)," Sam replied.

"Yeah, I know. Hey, Michele was in Memphis when they had that earthquake," Brian sent.

"Oh my, is she all right?" Sam asked.

"Yeah, just a little shaken up. No pun intended. :)," he replied.

Sam smiled and shook her head. She was glad that Brian was in a seemingly good mood.

"I know that we haven't talked about this much, but have you considered preparing for an emergency?" Sam texted.

There was a pause for several minutes. She hoped that she didn't make him mad by asking. She told everyone in her family to get prepared for the worst, but most of them didn't pay attention. Her oldest brother, Ralph, who lived in the Upper Peninsula of Michigan, was the only one who heeded her words. Sometimes texting could be tricky. She preferred face-to-face communication because there was less chance of being misunderstood.

Sam sat there for another ten minutes and decided that she would go to bed. As she stood up, her phone dinged, indicating a new text had come in.

"No, I haven't done anything, but I'm starting to think you're right," Brian replied. "Where do you think I should start?"

"Brian, I would start by having a couple weeks' supply of food and water," Sam replied. "After that, you should think about self-defense and shelter."

"What do you mean by self-defense?" Brian asked.

"Well, getting a gun might be a good start. Obviously, you need to be careful with it," Sam replied. "If Mom and Dad had a fireplace, I would recommend stocking up on wood. It will get cold if we lose power."

"Okay, I need to think about all this," Brian replied. "I should get in bed. I have a long day of work tomorrow. Good night!"

"Good night!" Sam replied.

Sam didn't expect to hear any more from Brian that night but waited for a few minutes before putting her phone away.

As Sam got ready for bed, she wondered if the rest of her family would consider preparing for the worst now that they had seen the results of the terror attacks. Tomorrow she would contact them and make sure that they were prepared. She said a quick prayer, thanking God for her family and wishing them health and safety.

Chapter 80

Nigel

Nigel spent several nights alone at the compound near Detroit after carrying out the attacks in Washington, DC. There were a dozen men and women there working on various tasks. Some were responsible for the care of those in the compound while others were preparing for the next wave of attacks. No one had yet heard from Ali, and Nigel was getting anxious. No one shared their concerns, but he thought that others probably shared his anxiety.

On the fifth night since his return to the compound, Nigel was awakened by the sound of someone knocking on his door. He looked at the clock and noticed that it was 3:33 a.m. For a slight moment, he thought that time seemed weird. He rubbed the sleep from his eyes and got up to answer the door. When he opened it, he was relieved to see Ali there, smiling. It was a rare occasion to witness Ali smiling.

"Come in! Come in!" Nigel exclaimed.

Ali gave Nigel a short hug and patted him on the back. "You've done marvelous work for Allah, my brother!" Ali exclaimed.

"Thank you, sir," Nigel replied humbly.

"We have the Americans confused and on the ropes," Ali started. "It's almost time that we put the final nail in the coffin, my friend."

"Allahu Akbar!" Nigel exclaimed with some excitement.

"Yes! Yes! Allahu Akbar!" Ali repeated.

"Ali, if I may ask," Nigel began, "where have you been? We were expecting you a few days ago. Some of us began to get concerned."

"Yes, yes. Well, I was delayed," Ali said. He paused for a moment, as if contemplating how much he should share. "More about that later! But for now, we must plan! Get dressed and meet me at the central hall."

"Yes! I'll be there in a moment," Nigel replied.

Ali left Nigel's small one-room cabin and disappeared into the night. While Nigel got dressed and pulled on his boots, he wondered what had delayed Ali.

"Had he been detained by the authorities, or did something else occupy his time?" he wondered aloud.

A few hours later, Nigel left the meeting concerned about his next attack. He still wasn't ready to die. He felt like he had much to do, and this attack would be dangerous. The National Football League was planning to have the Super Bowl in San Francisco in a couple of weeks. Ali apparently knew about the coming attacks there and put together a plan in Detroit, which had been declared the alternative location in case San Francisco wasn't able to hold the event.

Nigel was surprised that the NFL was still planning to hold the game, especially after what happened in Washington, DC. Apparently, the president of the United States asked that they hold the game anyway. It seemed like it was a show of defiance to the terrorists.

Since all of Nigel's original team had been either killed or captured in Washington, DC, he was forced to build a new team from the people who were left at the compound. He had just over a week to get them trained for the job. Ali arranged for Nigel's team to be part of the halftime crew. They would be responsible for moving the center portion of the stage into place at halftime. They were to place two cylinders of blue napalm within the stage section. They were built to look just like the hydraulic cylinders that were used to raise and lower the stage. The amount of blue napalm was double the amount used in Nashville. The plan was to have the device go off right in the middle of the halftime performance.

Ali estimated a casualty count of fifty thousand or more. The sheer number of deaths shook Nigel to the bone, but his primary concern was his ability to get out of the arena and out of the blast radius before the device was detonated. He wondered if he was living the last days of his life.

CHAPTER 81

Washington, D. C.

The president sat at his desk on Air Force One. For the most part, he was in continuous flight since the attack on the White House. He and his cabinet had barely escaped with their lives. He was thankful that his wife and children were at Camp David during the attack, and he was grateful to have them with him now.

It would be months before the White House would be usable again. He didn't expect to move back in before his term was up. They expected the United States Capitol building to be a complete loss, and the current plan was to tear down what remained and rebuild from scratch. That would take more than a year to complete. Only thirteen senators survived the attack, with an additional sixteen who were not in attendance during the attack. That left twenty-nine senators out of the one hundred who were in office. The attack left the United States government vulnerable. The current legislative body, which was scattered throughout the country, was working to develop new rules for the creation of legislation that would be in place until all the open seats were filled.

A small group of legislators—including the speaker of the House, the majority leader and minority leader of the House, along with three ranking members of the remaining Senate—

was meeting with the vice president in his residence located within the US Naval Observatory in Washington, D.C.

The speaker of the House suggested that the entire government move to the old NORAD operations center in Cheyenne Mountain.

"That's a little extreme, don't you think?" the vice president asked, responding to the speaker's suggestion.

"John, we are at war!" the speaker exclaimed. "Right now, we are the most vulnerable we've been since the Civil War!"

John Harris was the vice president of the United States. Before the attacks on Washington, DC, he had considered a run for the office of president since the current president was near the end of his second term. But now, his perspective had changed. He didn't think he was ready to give his life to his country anymore, if it actually could mean giving his life.

"Bob, I know that we are at war, but what will the people think if we go and hide in a Cold War bunker?" he questioned.

Bob Daniels was the recently elected speaker of the House. He was young and full of energy. He had moved up quickly in the ranks of the Republican party. He truly was the voice of the conservative movement in the United States.

The minority leader of the House of Representatives agreed with his fellow Democrat and made a plea to avoid using Cheyenne Mountain. He suggested that the legislative body move to Philadelphia in the short term or possibly New York City.

The majority leader of the House of Representatives was leaning toward a Philadelphia location. He silently wondered if there was a technological solution that would allow them to work remotely from their individual home states, but he didn't think any of them would buy in.

Howard Stark, the Democrat senator from Michigan, sat there in silence, considering the options and finally spoke up, "If we need to be in a single location, I vote for Philadelphia. New York City seems like it will continue to be a target. But I have a thought that might help keep the terrorists on their heels." Howard paused. "Have you ever considered allowing us to telecommute?" he asked. "The technology is there to support virtual meetings, and with all of us spread out across the country, it will make it difficult for the terrorists to target a single location."

The majority leader nodded in agreement, but inside, he was kicking himself. *Why do you question yourself?* the majority leader thought.

The room was silent for a few moments until the vice president spoke up. "We will have to work out the security issues inherent in video transmissions over the Internet, but that seems like a good idea," the vice president said. "But I would also propose that we meet in Philadelphia once a month or so. This will also give us the perception of actually doing something. Bob, what do you think? Maybe we use Philadelphia for our monthly meeting place, but at the same time, we set up an emergency location in Cheyenne Mountain if it looks like things are getting worse. What say you?" the vice president asked. "What say all of you?" he addressed the rest of the room.

"Okay, that makes sense," the speaker replied. "Good idea, Howard! Let's have a preliminary vote and then send it out to everyone else."

The vote was unanimous. Before ending the meeting, they split up the tasks among themselves to ensure that their plan could get executed as soon as possible.

Bob Daniels was profoundly impacted by how easy it was to come to a decision. *If only it was this easy all the time*, he thought to himself.

"I'll touch base with the president and let him know our plan," the vice president said. He too was amazed at how quickly they had come to a consensus. Even though the room was split down the middle according to party lines, they were able to finally agree unanimously. *Maybe this attack would end up being a good thing*, he thought to himself as the wheels began to turn in his mind.

CHAPTER 82

Santiago, Chile

For almost three weeks, Dr. Stephen Weinstein of the United States Geological Survey had been on-site with his team at a mountain village about twenty miles from Mount Tupungatito. All signs pointed to an eminent eruption from the volcano, but then everything went completely quiet. There had not been any seismic activity in the last five days, and his team was totally confused.

The team received news of the New Year's Eve terrorist attacks in America and France. They also heard about the tsunamis in Honolulu and San Francisco. The news regarding the terror attacks in Washington, DC, concerned them the most. The team had taken a vote and decided that rather than go home, they would stay another week to observe the mountain. If nothing happened soon, they would get back to Santiago and then make the long trip home.

It was difficult to keep the team's spirits up, especially when nothing was going on with the volcano. Dr. Stephen Weinstein was sitting at his desk, wondering what was going on with Tupungatito. Across the room, Tracy, one of his team members, was monitoring the seismograph and stirring her tea. From a distance, she seemed as bored as he was. The rest of the team had gone out to stretch their legs. It was getting close to dinnertime, and Stephen was getting hungry.

He was about to tell Tracy to take a break when the red light on the seismograph lit up. The light was set to turn on when a seismic event that registered greater than 3.0 on the Richter scale occurred. The warning beep would go off when it hit 4.0, and the siren would follow at 5.0.

Tracy noticed the light about the same time that Stephen did. A moment later, the machine began to beep. At that, Tracy turned to look at Stephen. Her eyebrows raised, and a smile started to appear on her lips. Geologists tend to get excited about seismic events. Stephen felt his heart rate increase a bit. He was getting up to go to the door and signal the rest of the team when the siren went off. It was wired to sound outside as well, so the team would be on their way soon.

Instead of going outside, Stephen walked over to where Tracy was, by the seismograph, to look at the readings. The machine showed an ever-increasing scribble of lines as the event increased. The digital readout currently read 5.5, but it was increasing.

As the team burst through the door, the seismograph registered 6.2. That qualified this as a significant event. The peak of Tupungatito could be viewed by the naked eye from outside, but the video camera that was placed on the roof of their building provided a better view because it was magnified by four times. They watched as steam and ash began to vent out of the volcano's crater. The ice cap that was there moments ago was disappearing at an alarming rate. Everyone could feel the energy in the room explode.

The earthquake dissipated after about thirty seconds of activity, and then the plume that was coming from the volcano stopped.

The room became still, and everyone watched the video screen. After a couple of minutes, all the bound-up energy that the team held in seemed to be sucked from the room. They had waited a long time for the volcano to erupt, and the letdown was just too much to handle. Cal and Ben left the building in a state that resembled depression. Tracy and Joe stayed to monitor the machines, and Stephen stood back and wondered at it all. He was hoping for an eruption because that was why they were in Chili. However, the potential devastation to the local population was a concern for him. He didn't want anyone to die, but without eruptions, they wouldn't be able to collect data; and without data, they wouldn't be able to warn people about potential eruptions.

Stephen's stomach reminded him that he had been hungry before the earthquake, so he decided to go to the refrigerator and grab a frozen burrito. He laughed at the idea of a frozen burrito in the middle of the mountains, but there he was, heating up the frozen treat in a microwave. The only sound in the room was the hum of the microwave.

Then Stephen felt a shudder. It wasn't a physical shudder but more like a feeling or intuition. He knew that something big was about to happen. A moment later, the microwave dinged, letting him know that the burrito was ready—and then the earth let him know that the volcano was ready.

The initial reading was 6.1, and the video screen showed another strong plume being vented from the crater. Cal and Ben came rushing back in. A moment later, the seismograph went crazy, and the mountain blew!

There was very little video of Mount Saint Helen's blast, but this made that look like a small eruption. The history of Mount Tupungatito was an explosive one, but this eruption was clearly greater than any recorded in the modern era in this part of the world.

Stephen looked at the monitor, and it showed a 7.9 reading. The initial blast had widened the length of the crater by over 50 percent. Stephen was relieved to find out that the blast mostly went in the southern direction, toward the uninhabited mountain valley. The pyroclastic flow rushed over the edge of the crater and moved southward at an estimated speed of 400 mph. It would destroy everything in its path and would extend ten to fifteen miles away.

The team was getting a large amount of data, and their mood increased by tenfold. The seismic activity decreased but was still hanging around the 3.5 range. The volcano was venting a massive amount of ash, and from a secondary camera, the team got a view of lava flowing out of the southern end of the crater. The camera was zoomed to its max, and the quality of the image wasn't great, but it was clearly lava flowing down the mountainside.

The team was engrossed in all the activity around Tupungatito when the seismic warning siren went off again. It registered an initial 5.8 reading, which soon increased to 7.3.There wasn't any visible change to Tupungatito, so it was unclear what was going on. Then Ben asked that they pan the secondary camera fifteen degrees to the north. As they panned, a new plume became visible. Stephen immediately rushed to his computer to determine what volcanic mountain lay over there. After a few minutes, he discovered El Plomo, but it had been dormant throughout modern history. Stephen couldn't find record of it ever erupting.

They didn't have a great view of the plume as it was blocked by other mountains; but an eruption of this type, including two separate volcanic systems, was unprecedented. Stephen decided that it was time to place a call to the USGS.

"Stephen, I get what you are saying," his supervisor said on the satellite phone, "but we have something big getting ready to go up here."

Stephen told him about both El Plomo and Tupungatito erupting. He told him that the data they were getting was incredible, but in the end, it didn't matter.

"Stephen, listen. I think that the Valles Caldera is showing signs of waking up," his supervisor said.

"Valles?" Stephen questioned.

At that, most of his team turned to look at him. Some of them had a concerned look on their faces. The Valles Caldera was located in Northwest New Mexico. It was considered an active caldera, but the only activity that has been recorded was the hot spring activity to the west of Santa Fe.

"Yes, Valles. I need you in Albuquerque in five days," his supervisor said.

Stephen hung up the phone and explained the situation to his team. Most were somewhat disappointed to go now that they were having activity, but the thought of the Valles Caldera blowing was crazy.

It would take a lot of hard work and some good luck, but they would leave Santiago two days after the call from USGS and would make it to Albuquerque with time to spare. They thought that they had left the chance of a lifetime, but little did they know that eventually they would witness something that had never been seen by mankind.

CHAPTER 83

Christopher

Chris and Sara had spent the last couple of weeks poring through all the evidence from Ed's hideout in Paris. Most of it was coded, and the analysts were working on cracking the code. There were some vague ties to New York City, but those were speculative at best. Since they had run out of options, Chris decided that they needed to head to New York City to review what the FBI was calling the vest factory.

The file said that twenty-four vests were recovered from the house in Brooklyn. The explosive material that was found in the vests was something new. The street name was *blue napalm* because of its color and because it resembled napalm in the way it exploded, but this blue napalm was far more deadly than the original napalm.

The CIA and FBI both had their forensic teams working to identify the chemistry of the explosive so that they could develop a way to detect it. It had become clear that this material was used in all the New Year's Eve attacks in Paris, Nashville, and New York City. It was also used in the attacks in Washington, DC. This material seemed like it might be the only tie between all the attacks other than ISIS taking responsibility for each of them.

Chris and Sara walked through the house in Brooklyn where the vests were found. They didn't find anything new that hadn't already been discovered, but being in that house gave them more motivation for some reason. It was not like they needed much motivation, with everything that they had been through.

Chris and Sara decided that they would stop at a café and have some lunch before heading back to the FBI office downtown. The FBI had been nice enough to lend them some space so that they could help with the investigation.

"Sara, I hate to bring this up right now, but—"

"Yes, you are very cute!" Sara exclaimed with a broad smile.

Chris immediately flushed.

Since arriving in New York, Sara had quit hiding her feelings for Chris. They had only kissed on a couple of occasions, but Chris was beginning to have very strong feelings for Sara. He decided that he would move slower than he did with the other women he dated in the past.

Chris recalled going to dinner at a local Italian restaurant the night before. After two bottles of wine, their inhibitions had come down, and Chris remembered having a hard time not wanting her. After dinner, they walked back to the hotel. They walked through the lobby in silence and went straight to the elevator. Chris could distinctly remember the warm feeling in his face and not being sure where their relationship was heading, but he did not want to ruin it.

Chris remembered reaching the elevator and the door opening as he pressed the call button. The elevator was empty, and the door seemed to take forever to close. When the elevator door finally closed, Sara launched herself into Chris's arms. He had been acutely aware of the softness of her lips against his and the eagerness of her mouth. They continued to kiss until the door opened on the third floor. They stopped kissing and were shocked to see an elderly couple in the opening. The woman smiled shyly, and the old man raised his eyebrows.

Chris and Sara separated and chuckled a bit as the couple entered the elevator. They rode the elevator the rest of the way to the sixth floor in silence. When the door opened, the older couple moved aside so that Chris and Sara could get out of the elevator. Sara grabbed Chris's hand and led them down the hall. When they reached the door to her room, she tipped her head up and pulled his face to hers.

Chris recalled the conversation they had outside her room.

———◆◆◆———

"I really like you, Chris," Sara said after they ended the embrace. "I have for a long time, probably since we met."

Chris smiled broadly at her revelation.

"But I need for this to go slow. I'm not one to simply jump into bed with any guy that I like," she said.

Chris could remember her face going red. Chris's smile wavered a bit, and for a moment, Sara wondered if he expected her to sleep with him.

"Sara, I'm glad you said that," Chris said. Her smile went flat, and he hurried to finish. "I really like you too!" he exclaimed. "Ten years ago, I probably would have tried to coax you into the room, but I don't want that with you."

Her look changed for the worse, and he remembered being visibly rattled.

"I mean, I do want that. I so want that!" Chris exclaimed. Nothing that he said seemed to help him get out of the hole he was digging for himself.

"It's just that," Chris remembered saying, "I love you!" He ended up blurting his feelings out before he thought about what he was saying. He recalled becoming so rattled that he didn't know what to do.

Sara's demeanor stiffened immediately, as if from shock, but then quickly softened. Sara's smile started out small and grew until it filled her entire face. Her beautiful blue eyes held his gaze, and he knew it before she had a chance to say a word.

"I love you too!" Sara whispered as she melted into him.

The memory of her words still put a smile on his face. His arms engulfed her completely, and they held each other for a long time. Finally she pulled back slightly and leaned in for another kiss. This time, Chris gently laid his hand on her cheek and pulled her closer. Never in his prior life had he felt the way he felt that night. After a few more moments, he kissed her forehead and excused himself before going back to his room. That memory would last a lifetime for Chris. He hadn't slept a wink that night as he remembered the taste of her lips and the smell of her perfume.

Back in the café, Chris looked to his left and to his right, as if to see if anyone heard her. He made a face as if to shush her and then smiled. "Well, I'm not the only one," Chris replied, which brought a big smile to Sara's face. "Okay, we have to get to work now. What I was going to say before I was so rudely interrupted," he said playfully, "was that in Paris, when Ed mentioned the Mahdi, you had a look of understanding. I wanted to understand what it is that you know."

At the mention of the Mahdi, Sara's demeanor changed completely. It was as if Chris had revealed her greatest fear. Sara fidgeted in her chair for a few moments and then cast her gaze directly at Chris. He could see fear and sorrow in her eyes.

"So you know that I am fluent in Arabic, right?" Sara asked.

Chris nodded in affirmation.

"Well, I learned Arabic in college, but then I went to the country of Jordan for a summer to learn more about Islamic cultures and to intermingle with the Muslim population," she continued with a pause. "I chose Jordan because it was relatively safe there, and the sharia customs weren't as harsh as they were in other Islamic countries.

"My girl friend Michele and I decided to travel together that summer after graduation. She studied education and was going to start her new teaching job in the fall. I had been accepted to the CIA academy and was going to start in the fall as well, so we decided to take the summer off and travel a bit. I had convinced her that Jordan was the place that we should start.

"We had only been in the country for a week when we were confronted by a group of Muslim men. We were on our way back to the hotel after dinner when they cornered us on the street. I think there were five of them, but it's hard to remember. They were yelling crude comments in Arabic. Some of the words I didn't understand, but I knew the basic meaning of their threats. One had said that they should rape us right there on the street. I knew that because we were women, we had virtually no rights. The added fact that we were non-Muslims basically gave them the right to do whatever they wanted to us.

"One advanced upon Michele and grabbed her and held her against his body. His hands were all over her, and I yelled at him to stop. They were a little surprised that I could speak Arabic, but it didn't stop them. Another grabbed me, and they were about to drag us into the alley when Michele bit the man who held her in the arm. She bit down hard enough to draw blood. His anger was so fierce that he grabbed her by the hair and smashed her head into the cement wall of the building. She immediately lost consciousness, and I continued to scream.

"My screams were heard by three large men who could have been American, but I never learned where they were from. Regardless, they didn't take too kindly to five Muslim men beating on two small women. They charged at the group of Muslim men and started beating them. The one man who held Michele was beaten senseless and was bleeding from multiple locations on his face and head.

"After the Muslim men fled, dragging their unconscious friend down the road, the three large men helped us to our hotel room. They recommended that we don't go to the hospital unless it was absolutely necessary. One seemed to know basic first aid and did what he could for Michele. She was conscious by the time they left us, and I was so thankful that they showed up when they did. Michele and I wouldn't be alive today if it weren't for them," Sara finished.

"Wow, that is an incredible story!" Chris exclaimed. "I'm so sorry that that happened to you." Then he asked, "But what does that have to do with the Mahdi?"

"Oh, right," Sara replied, "I forgot. Before the three men left, they said that it wouldn't be safe for us on the streets anymore and that we should probably get out of the country and pretty much stay away from any Muslim country.

"I didn't like the idea of leaving so soon, so I asked them why, and they said that the Mahdi had declared war on all infidels. I asked him who the Mahdi was, and he said he didn't know who the Mahdi was but that he was the supreme leader of the Islamic world. He said that no one except his closest advisors knew what he looked like or where he was. He apparently was still underground but was working to build his political power. It seemed like it was enough for all Muslims, especially the radical ones, to accept the fact that he was alive and in control," Sara said then paused.

"Okay, so I don't get it," Chris started. "Some mystery man is out there calling the shots for all Muslims?"

"Yeah, it didn't make sense to me either," Sara replied, "so I did a little research." She seemed to be thinking and organizing her thoughts, so Chris waited. After a moment, she continued, "The Mahdi is from Islamic end-times prophecy. He is prophesized to come back and be the savior of the world."

"So the Mahdi is Jesus?" Chris asked. He knew right away that he was wrong because of the look of horror on Sara's face.

"Oh no!" Sara exclaimed. "No, he is nothing like that!"

Chris could tell that she was struggling.

"I think he is actually the exact opposite of Jesus," Sara continued. "You see, Muslims believe in Jesus too. They just don't believe that He is God. They believe that He was simply a man who was also a prophet. They also believe that Jesus will come back before the Mahdi makes himself known. They believe that Jesus will bow down to the Mahdi and proclaim Islam as the true religion and Allah to be the true God."

Chris was confused and wondered how there could be two different Jesuses. It didn't make any sense to him. Sara could see that he was trying to process everything.

"Okay, I know that it's confusing, but let me try to explain a few more things, and then I'll explain why this applies to what is going on in today's world. So I did some research, and in Islamic end-times prophecy, there are three main players: the Mahdi, the Muslim Jesus, and a character called ad-Dajjal. This ad-Dajjal is the character who is trying to defeat the Mahdi. As I said before, the Muslim Jesus is supposed to support the Mahdi.

"Here is the kicker. If you look at Christian end-times prophecy, there are three main players too: the Antichrist, the false prophet, and Jesus. This is our Jesus, not the Muslim Jesus. There is much evidence that points to the Muslim Mahdi being the same as the Christian Antichrist, and the Muslim Jesus being the same as the false prophet, and the ad-Dajjal being the same as the real Jesus," Sara said and paused to let it sink in a bit.

"Sara, I am not well-read when it comes to the Bible," Chris said. "I get that the Antichrist is the bad guy, but I really don't understand the significance."

"Basically, the Antichrist is sent by Satan into the world prior to the return of Jesus," Sara explained. "He is the ultimate in evil. He will lead many astray and will rule most of the world up until the return of Jesus." Sara thought for a moment and then continued, "Jesus said that the last days would be like the days of Noah."

She saw more confusion on Chris's face but motioned that she would explain. "In the days of Noah, the world was a wicked place, and God was ready to destroy everyone and everything on the earth. But Noah was found to be worthy, and God told him to build the ark so that he and his family would be saved from the flood. God let Noah and his family live to repopulate the world.

"So back to what Jesus said, He said the world in the last days would be like the days of Noah, and he meant that the world would be a wicked place. Obviously, the Christians wouldn't be wicked, but they would become targets for the wicked. The Bible also talks about Christians being killed because of their love of Jesus." Sara paused for a moment as if to recall one more bit of information.

"I can't recall where it says this, but the Bible talks about God creating a great delusion on all the non-Christians in the end-times. That's not quite right. I think the Jewish people will be okay. Anyway, this delusion will cause people to believe in the miracles performed by the Antichrist and the false prophet," Sara said with a pause. She could tell that Chris had a question, so she waited.

"Okay, so the Antichrist is Satan's number one dude, and he will lead many away from Christ. I get that," Chris said then paused. "But who is this false prophet?" he questioned.

"The book of Revelation, the last book in the Bible, talks about two beasts. These beasts are symbolic for the Antichrist and the false prophet. The false prophet is the second beast. He is given power by the first beast, the Antichrist. The false prophet will make the world bow down to the Antichrist. He will perform miracles, like raining fire down on the earth. But most importantly, he will force everyone who is not saved to take the mark of the beast. It is a mark that will be on your right hand or forehead. Without this mark, you won't be able to buy or sell anything. By taking the mark, you damn your soul forever!" Sara exclaimed.

"So the false prophet, I believe, will come into the world and will claim to be Jesus. He will lead many away from Christianity and trick them into worshiping the first beast, the Antichrist. Jesus told the disciples that if someone says that Jesus is in the desert, not to believe them. If someone says that Jesus is in the inner room, not to believe them. Jesus said that His second coming will be visible by the entire world. He will come on the clouds, and we will all know that He is here. Yet the Bible also says that many will be led astray," Sara concluded.

It was a lot of information for Chris to absorb. He decided then that he would pick up a Bible on the way back to the hotel and do a little research for himself.

"So let's get back to what Ed said in Paris," Chris replied. "Ed believed that he was working for this Mahdi. We don't know that this Mahdi is truly the one, do we?"

"Obviously, we can't know without doing more research," Sara answered. "We don't know if Ed ever had any face-to-face meeting with this Mahdi either."

"I'm going to contact Langley and see if we can get some information on Ed's travel history for the last several years," Chris stated. "That might give us a list of suspects that we can track down."

They finished lunch and decided that they should head back to the FBI office. As they drove, Chris wondered about Sara's knowledge of end-times prophecy. He wondered if it was her brush with death in Jordan or something else that led her to it. He always believed in God and prayed on occasion, mostly when he needed something. He almost never went to church and wondered how he would be categorized by God, as a Christian or not. He had always heard about born-again Christians but really had no idea what that meant.

Am I a Christian? he wondered. I don't know. He looked over at Sara briefly as he drove. He wanted to ask her more about being a Christian but was afraid to ask. He assumed that she was a Christian, but he could not be sure. *But her passion was so strong when she talked about Jesus, the Antichrist, and the end-times.*

As they pulled into the parking garage, he decided that he would ask Sara more questions after dinner. Little did Chris know that his life was about to change forever.

CHAPTER 84

Mediterranean Sea

After being attacked by the Chinese submarine, the *USS George H.W. Bush* aircraft carrier was forced to anchor off the coast of Israel near Tel-Aviv so that they could begin repairs. The ships that made up the rest of the carrier group spent their days patrolling the area on high alert. Their primary mission was to ensure that repairs could be made to the carrier. The initial assessment was that it would be months before the carrier was ready for combat duty.

Seaman Robert Williams found himself distracted the past few days. The attack on San Francisco affected him personally as it was likely that his fiancée was killed by the tsunami. No word had come from Bridget or her family. Many of his shipmates lost loved ones there as well. Communications out of San Francisco had been few, even weeks after the attack.

"How could you allow this to happen?" he questioned God. "Millions of innocent people lost."

His pain was unbearable, and not knowing for sure only made it worse. He had gone to talk to the chaplain but only got into an argument with him when the chaplain said, "God has a plan." He couldn't imagine any of this being part of

God's plan, and if it was, he didn't want any part of a god that slaughtered millions of innocent people.

When the news about the attacks on Washington, DC, reached the ship, the crew was ready to enact revenge on the enemy in any manner possible. A second United States aircraft carrier group was ordered into the Mediterranean Sea. This would allow the United States to continue operations in the Middle East, as well as deal with any new developments with Russia. The president of the United States had gone on television and said that they would continue their missions against ISIS in Syria. He reported that the American's primary military base in Iraq had been destroyed by the Russians and that the United States had retaliated, but both countries had agreed to not escalate. The president confirmed rumors that a cease-fire had also been declared with China.

The president said that all troops stationed in Afghanistan had been called home. The president felt that it was necessary to have additional resources back to protect the homeland. In the end, it took a couple of months before all military personnel were brought home. Shortly after the United States left, Afghanistan was abandoned to the Taliban and al-Qaeda. Both groups would pledge their allegiance to ISIS. The vacuum created by the departure of the Americans would be filled by the worst type of terrorists. Soon al-Qaeda and ISIS would build another stronghold in Afghanistan.

Months before the attacks on the United States and Paris, Turkey and Russia had taken a more active role in the fight against ISIS. As time went on, it became clear to the world that Russia solely supported the existing Syrian government, and Turkey openly supported ISIS and the Syrian rebels. For years, Turkey had been buying black market oil from ISIS and had effectively funded ISIS terror activity throughout the globe. Russia had begun destroying the ISIS oil-production facilities and distribution systems. These attacks disrupted the flow of cheap oil into Turkey, and tensions increased even higher between the two countries.

Finally, a Russian fighter-bomber was shot down by the Turkish air defense when it crossed into Turkish airspace. Russia suffered other losses at the hands of the Americans because of strikes on the American military base near Baghdad. Tensions were high between Russia and the United States, but for the time being, Russia had agreed to a truce.

Turkey set up a blockade in Istanbul and didn't allow Russian ships out of the Black Sea. Because the Russian military base in Syria was destroyed by the Americans, the Russians were finding it increasingly difficult to engage in the war within Syria. Syrian government positions were shrinking on a daily basis, and as a result, ISIS was gaining control over most of the country. Damascus was in danger of being overrun. Turkey established a no-fly zone in the northern one-third of Syria. Three more Russian fighter-bombers were almost shot out of the sky by the Turkish fighters. The Russian jets turned away moments before they were fired upon. The Russians had threatened the use of nuclear weapons on ISIS if Turkey didn't back down. It seemed that the use of nuclear weapons against North Korea by the United States had set a new standard, and global tensions grew further.

The environment in Syria was about to turn into an all-out war between Russia and Turkey. Russia began building up troops near the northern border of Georgia, and a new military base had been set up in Tabriz, Iran. Turkey responded by moving troops near the southern border of Georgia. The president of Georgia called on the United Nations to step in, but that body was bogged down in bureaucracy as usual.

United States' military bases throughout Europe had been placed on high alert because there were concerns of an escalation between Turkey and Russia. Because Turkey was part of NATO, there was a chance that the United States and Europe could be pulled into the conflict between Turkey and Russia. NATO troop numbers increased in Germany and Poland and throughout other European countries. The United States secretly placed new nuclear assets in Europe as well. Russia had already threatened to use nukes in the Middle East. If things escalated between NATO and Russia, the United States might have to protect Europe with nuclear weapons for the first time in history.

As all of this was going on between Turkey and Russia, the world had forgotten about Iran. They were about to make history and begin fulfilling biblical prophecy.

CHAPTER 85

General Hasim

G eneral Hasim received word from the Ayatollah that the time to move was upon him. The American military was distracted on three fronts with the North Koreans, the Chinese, and the Russians. They would not have the will, nor the means, to stop any advances toward their goal of a new Persian Empire.

The country of Iraq was controlled by the Iranian military, and an Iranian advance into Syria would initially be camouflaged as attacks against ISIS. By the time the world realized what was going on, it would be too late for them to do anything. The most difficult component of this war would be against the Saudi Arabians. The Saudi Air Force was made of American-built F-16s and was superior to the Iranian Air Force.

Hasim gave the word for the invasion to begin. A fleet of submarines and warships left the naval base located in the town of Bandar-e Abbas on the southern coast of Iran. Their mission was to create a blockade at the southern end of the Persian Gulf. This fleet would also serve as a countermeasure to the unlikely attack launched by the United Arab Emirates and other Sunni coastal nations.

A second fleet was positioned off the coast of Yemen since the Yemen insurgence had started a few years earlier. The primary purpose of this second fleet was to support the Iranian-backed rebels there. Upon his command, the majority of this fleet would move into position at the narrow straits near the southern end of the Red Sea. Within a week, Iran would control the flow of oil coming out of the Middle East. The rest of this second fleet was made up of mostly transport ships containing more than fifteen thousand troops and one hundred tanks. These troops would land in the coastal city of Aden and move to secure Yemen. Once Yemen was secure, the vast majority of these troops would move into Saudi Arabia with a final destination of Mecca. If everything went as planned, the Saudi capital city of Riyadh would have already surrendered.

Since the American military base in Baghdad was destroyed, the Iranian military had the opportunity to build up a force of fifty thousand soldiers near Baghdad. Hasim had sent word for them to begin advancing on ISIS positions to the north and west of Baghdad. Another one hundred thousand troops would arrive in Baghdad from Shush in a matter of days. A second deployment of nearly one hundred and fifty thousand troops, including three tank brigades, entered Iraq near the southern border town of Basra. They would hold strategic positions on the Shatt al-Arab river leading to the Persian Gulf and continue on into Kuwait. The incursion into Kuwait would lead to war with the Saudis, but General Hasim was prepared for that.

Months ago, a million reserve forces had been called up to prepare. Half of these forces would follow the primary army and serve as security forces, as well as reserves. The other half would mobilize throughout Iran and serve as a defense should the Iranian homeland be attacked.

The war for the conquest of the Middle East had begun, and Iran proved itself to be the Persian ram found in the book of Daniel chapter 8.

CHAPTER 86

South China Sea

The destruction of the two North Korean military bases by American nuclear bombs had infuriated the president of North Korea. He ramped up his campaign against the United States naval forces located in the region. The *USS Ronald Reagan* carrier group had suffered some losses, but in return, the majority of the North Korean naval forces were destroyed. They were no match for the superior power of the United States Navy.

North Korea pleaded with the Chinese to intercede, but to no avail. North Korea threatened to launch an invasion into South Korea, but that threat was immediately rebuked with a warning from the United States that further attacks would be retaliated in the extreme. These threats held off the North Koreans for some time, but it would only be a matter of months before the situation in the region would flare up again.

CHAPTER 87

United States

The United States lost much of its influence over the rest of the world because of the policies that the president pursued throughout his two terms in office. The devastating attacks in Washington, DC, New York, Nashville, Hawaii, and San Francisco alone could bring the financial solvency of the United States government to an end. The damages had already been estimated in the trillions of dollars, and it was unlikely that the money to rebuild everything could be found. Hard decisions would have to be made.

The stock market crash that began shortly after the New Year's Eve attacks had already cut the global stock prices by slightly more than 50 percent. The Dow Jones Industrial Average had dipped below five thousand for a day but had resurged to just under six thousand a couple of days later. The market hadn't been this low since the crash of 2007 to 2008. The last time the market crashed, the government bailed out several large banks and a car company. This time, no funds were available, and it was likely that many companies would fail.

The financial segments of the stock market had plummeted, and housing was sure to follow suit within months. Gas and oil prices in the United States began to rise on global demand but stopped around $50 per barrel. The increased production of gas and oil within the United States kept local prices down. However, the Iranian blockade of the Persian Gulf and Red Sea had prices outside the United States reaching $65 per barrel. This was nearly a doubling of the price within the time frame of a few weeks. The United States president had put a referendum on all oil and gas exports until the Iranian blockade was resolved. All funding to other countries, except Israel, also was halted. The Americans simply didn't have the wherewithal to continue supporting the entire world.

The Iranian blockade and advances throughout the Middle East clearly pointed toward the Iranians' desire to completely dominate the Middle East.

The new President of the United States was inaugurated, and he now faced the most difficult presidency in the history of the country. Fortunately, the election from the previous November had been complete prior to the New Year's Eve attacks. If they hadn't been, who knew what the previous president would have done. Those elections also filled fifteen of the Senate seats that had been vacated by the tragic attack on the United States Capitol building. Many more seats would need to be filled, but hopefully, the new president would be able to help make that happen soon. The previous president made many mistakes during his presidency. Many of those mistakes helped move the world into the position that it was in, and the decisions that were made in the last week of his presidency could seal the fate of the United States, unless the new president was able to act quickly.

The world was now vulnerable because of the leadership vacuum that the last president had created. Afghanistan had turned into a terrorist safe haven again, but the troops who returned home gave the United States government a chance to provide security for its people.

The new president had ordered fifty thousand troops to be deployed to the southern border of the United States adjacent to Mexico. He ordered all illegal immigrants who were already in the country and those discovered crossing the border to be immediately deported. Congress finally voted to build a wall along the complete length of the border from Texas to California. Dozens of temporary prisons were built along the border of Texas and Arizona. Initially, California had refused to implement the new deportation orders, but the president strong-armed them into conceding.

The new president found immediate approval for these actions within all regions of the country. With the Congress in disarray, he took the opportunity to push his agendas. The American people immediately supported his harsh immigration policies because of their desire for more security. They raved about him bringing home the troops. This once globally minded country was quickly becoming isolationistic.

CHAPTER 88

Samantha

So much happened so fast for Sam. Just the day before, she and Rob had purchased several firearms. They purchased a .22-caliber rifle, along with one thousand rounds of ammunition, and a 12-gauge shotgun, along with four hundred rounds of ammunition. They also purchased a 9mm handgun for each of them. Rob picked a Glock double stack that held seventeen rounds. Sam picked a Beretta Nano, which was smaller and fit better in her hand. They purchased one thousand rounds of ammunition for the handguns.

After purchasing the guns, they spent some time shooting each of them at targets and getting used to the feel of each. Jacob and Isaac had both joined in the activity, and it seemed to give everyone peace of mind that they now had some protection. Sam hoped that she would never have to use the gun to protect her family, but she thought that she might be ready to do so if necessary.

With the boys in school and Rob back at work, Sam took this opportunity to continue her thoughts about the Ezekiel war.

"So I already figured out that Rosh does not represent Russia," Sam said to herself, "but that doesn't mean that Magog isn't Russia. Ford once said that he thought Magog was in Turkey." She would have to have Ford explain that.

Sam opened the Bible to Ezekiel 38:5 and began listing the nations involved in the war.

"Hmmm, Persia, Cush, and Put," Sam began. "Persia is obviously Iran, but what about Cush and Put?" She went to her computer and opened a web browser. After doing a quick search on Cush, she discovered that Cush was the region currently occupied by Sudan. She did the same for Put and found that it related to Libya.

"Interesting, all three nations have Islamic governments," Sam noted. She wrote down those three nations and their corresponding modern nations. She continued reading Ezekiel 38 and found Gomer, Beth Togarmah, and one more that she found interesting.

"Many nations with them?" she wondered aloud. "That could be anything." She decided to perform a web search on Gomer and Beth Togarmah. She found that Gomer was located in the northeast corner of modern-day Turkey, and Beth Togarmah was located in the southeast corner of modern-day Turkey.

"Interesting! Oh, I forgot about Meshech and Tubal," she stated. A search found many variations, but for the most part, Meshech was found to be located in the western portion of the modern-day country of Turkey. Tubal was found to be in the central southern portion of modern-day Turkey.

"Wow, many of these nations are found in Turkey," she stated aloud. "So if Gog is from Magog and is also the chief prince of Meshech and Tubal as Ezekiel 38:2 states, then I can see why Ford would think that Magog would be in Turkey, since both Meshech and Tubal are located there."

She smiled because she was talking to herself again and because she had learned so much. She did another search for Magog and got a ton of hits. Some websites pointed to

Russia, and a few pointed to Turkey, but there was just too much information to process in one night. It was time to e-mail Ford and ask why he thought Magog was located in modern-day Turkey.

CHAPTER 89

Ford

The new president had run on the platform of fixing all the things that his predecessor had broken, but upon entering office, he found new focus in the security of the country. Ford had voted for the president and, for the most part, wanted to support him. Ford didn't like that the president began pulling more power to himself almost immediately, but he understood how difficult this new president's job would be.

Ford decided to check his e-mail. He was surprised that, for the most part, life seemed to be rolling on as usual. People were definitely more apprehensive and tense, but that was understandable. Before looking at his e-mail, a story on his favorite news website caught his eye. The story said that the Eiffel Tower had finally collapsed. Ford clicked on the link to the video and found himself sick to his stomach after watching the iconic tower crash to the ground. So many things had changed in the world.

When he finally opened his e-mail, he saw the e-mail from Sam and immediately opened it. He wondered how she was doing.

Hey Ford,

I hope you and your family are doing okay. This has been a crazy month, hasn't it?

Anyway, I was thinking about Gog and Magog. I'm really close to being onboard with Magog not being Russia, but please explain to me why it is Turkey. Maybe an explanation as to why you think Gog is the Antichrist as well. LOL

Talk soon!

Samantha

Ford looked at the e-mail and smiled. He was glad that Sam was expanding her understanding of Ezekiel, and he was glad that he was able to help her in this regard. She had helped him in so many other ways. She taught him to listen to God. She taught him how God wanted them to share the Word.

Ford recalled what he knew about Ezekiel 38–39. He knew which nations would wage war against Israel as described in Ezekiel. He believed that Magog was located in the north central region of the modern-day nation of Turkey. He just needed to find the "proof" that he could share with Sam.

Ford opened the Bible and flipped to the book of Genesis chapter 9. The scripture told of Noah's three sons: Shem, Ham, and Japheth. In chapter 10, Ford read the genealogy of Noah's sons. Japheth had seven sons: Gomer, Magog, Madai, Javan, Tubal, Meshech, and Tiras. Ford found it interesting that some of these names were found in Ezekiel 38–39.

Ford had read several commentators on Ezekiel. Many of these concluded that the tribe of Magog had primarily lived in the north central region of Turkey during Ezekiel's lifetime. A few scholars from the AD first century had identified the areas north of the Black Sea as the homeland of the Magog people. Unfortunately, these scholars didn't take into account that the Magog people hadn't been in that region during Ezekiel's lifetime. Many of the commentators who held to the idea that Magog was Russia primarily used the scholars who documented the location of Magog during the first century. Ford realized that it was important to identify the homeland of the Magog people based on where they were during Ezekiel's lifetime several centuries earlier.

Ford considered Ezekiel 38:2 again: "Son of man, set your face against Gog, of the land of Magog, the chief prince of Meshech and Tubal; prophesy against him."

"If Gog is from Magog but also the chief prince of Meshech and Tubal...," Ford spoke aloud. He leaned back in his chair with his hands behind his head and thought for a moment. "How likely would it be that a leader of a nation north of the Black Sea would also be a leader of a pair of nations south of the Black Sea? In the time of Ezekiel, the region of Magog was ruled by the Babylonian Empire. The capital of that empire was, of course, Babylon, which is located in modern-day Iraq. Since Gog didn't live in Babylon and was a chief prince of Magog, Meshech, and Tubal, it seems clear that he wasn't the emperor back then," Ford said then paused.

Ford pulled up a map of the Black Sea region. There was so much distance between the regions north and south of the Black Sea. The distance on land from north to south was farther than the distance from Turkey to Babylon.

"It is unlikely that Gog would have claimed control over the areas north and south of the Black Sea. Magog had to be located in north central Turkey!" Ford exclaimed. "Meshech and Tubal would have been neighbors. The evidence seems clear to me."

Ford opened up his email again and began typing a letter to Sam.

CHAPTER 90

Samantha

Sam was still at her computer when she got Ford's e-mail.

That didn't take long, she thought. Sam read his e-mail with interest and concluded that he was probably right. "I guess I will have to send him that apple pie after all," she said aloud. She thought of the bet that they made many months before and began laughing out loud.

Ford's e-mail was short, and even though it identified Turkey as the region where Gog would come from, it didn't give her any proof that Gog was the Antichrist. So she wrote down her thoughts on what she knew about Gog.

"Okay, so the first thing I know is that Gog and a group of nations attack Israel," Sam said as she wrote it down. "The people of Israel will suffer distress at the hands of Gog," Sam paraphrased from Ezekiel 38:11–12.

"At that time, God will intervene, and there will be an earthquake that is felt by all the people and creatures of the earth," Sam read from Ezekiel 38:19–20.

"God will make himself known in the sight of many nations," Sam read from Ezekiel 38:23.

"God will make known his holy name and will no longer let his holy name be profaned!" Sam exclaimed as she read from Ezekiel 39:7. This last verse was so compelling for Sam. "God's name will no longer be profaned," she repeated.

CHAPTER 91

Ford

As Ford was thinking about shutting down his computer, he heard the familiar ding that told him that he had a new e-mail. He quickly opened the e-mail program and saw that it was from Samantha. Her e-mail discussed some verses from Ezekiel and how she was starting to believe that Gog and the Antichrist were the same.

"God's name will no longer be profaned, it says in Ezekiel 39:7," Ford read from Sam's e-mail. "If God's name will no longer be profaned, then how can any of the events found in the book of Revelation happen after the Ezekiel war?" she asked in her e-mail.

Ford read the question again and realized that she had answered the question that he had been trying to answer for months. He flipped between Ezekiel and Revelation and found two more pieces of evidence that virtually proved that Gog and the Antichrist were the same.

"In Ezekiel 38:19–20, there is an earthquake that is felt by all the inhabitants of the earth. Mountains are overturned, and cliffs crumble," he read aloud. "In Revelation 16:18–19, there is an earthquake that is so severe that no earthquake has ever occurred like it since man has been on earth. Every island fled away, and the mountains could not be found!" Ford exclaimed.

"Both earthquakes are of unspeakable power—how can they be different? The mountains are overturned and could not be found! Amazing!" Ford continued, "Ezekiel 40–43, the chapters after the war, talk about a new temple being built, and in Ezekiel 43:7, the Bible says, 'The house of Israel will never again defile my holy name—neither they nor their kings—by their prostitution and the lifeless idols of their kings in high places.' They can't defile God's name because all evil has been removed from the earth and Jesus reigns!

"Ezekiel 44–46 continues to describe the new laws for worship, and Ezekiel 47 talks about the river running through the temple." Ford flipped forward to Revelation and was amazed. "Revelation 21 is after the war of Armageddon and talks about a new Jerusalem. This seems to mirror the idea of a new temple."

"Revelation 22 talks about the river of life flowing through the middle of the great street of the city of Jerusalem. Isn't that just like Ezekiel 47?" Ford thought aloud. "That is too much coincidence for me. Gog has to be the Antichrist!"

Ford's body was still as he sat on his chair, but his mind was racing as he contemplated everything that he had just discovered. He found that the book of Daniel prophesied from what nation the Antichrist would arise. He discovered that Gog and the Antichrist were the same individual. He had almost assuredly determined that the first seal of Revelation had already been opened and that the Antichrist had been released upon the world. Ford recalled that the Persian ram found in the book of Daniel chapter 8 was tied to the rider on the red horse in the book of Revelation, who would be released with the opening of the second seal. This rider would take peace from the earth. All the recent news had been about the recent moves by Iran to control the Middle East.

"The Persian ram has begun its conquest! The second seal has been opened!" Ford exclaimed. "God be with us and keep us safe, for everything is about to change."

When the Lamb opened the second seal, I heard the second living creature say, "Come!" Then another horse came out, a fiery red one. Its rider was given power to take peace from the earth and to make men slay each other. To him was given a large sword.

—Revelation 6:3–4

CHAPTER 92

Nigel

Nigel and his team found their way out to midfield with the rest of the support staff. The stage was now in place, and within minutes, the halftime show would begin. Five minutes into the show, the device would detonate with a display of pyrotechnics, which would consume the entire stadium. Nigel and one of his team had slipped out the private exit at the north end of the stadium. As they approached their van, a security guard stopped them. Nigel could see that three other team members had already reached the van and were anxiously waiting for him to drive.

"Hey guys, what do you think of the game so far?" the security guard asked.

"I didn't get a chance to watch much of it," Nigel replied. He could tell that his partner was getting nervous. "We were working on the halftime-show setup," he added. He glanced at his watch, knowing that he had about two minutes to get out of the parking lot.

"Wow, that's kind of cool," the security guard started. "I've been out here the entire game. I've caught bits and pieces, but it looks like a good one."

"Yeah, too bad, man," Nigel started. "But hey, we gotta get going. You have a good one!" At that, he started walking toward the van with his partner.

"Yeah, you too!" the guard replied.

When he got to the van, he looked at his watch and noted that he had about thirty seconds before the device exploded. He started up the van, shifted the van in reverse, and then after completely pulling out of his parking spot, violently shifted the van into drive and stomped down on the accelerator.

"Hang on!" Nigel said as he approached the parking lot gate. He pressed down farther and crashed through the metal gate as another security guard dove out of the way. He turned left and then made a quick right onto Brush Street and headed north. He looked back and saw the guard yelling at him as the stadium exploded. Flames went through the roof and out of every exit. Nigel saw the security guard get thrown to the ground as he drove out of sight.

The death toll would reach 64,344, including several celebrities and the players from both teams. With nearly 130 million viewers, the people of the United States would truly be terrorized now. In the past two months, they had witnessed the destruction of Time's Square, Nashville, the White House, the United State's Capitol, Honolulu, San Francisco, and now the Super Bowl.

Nigel and his team made it back to the compound without incident. Nigel sat in his cabin waiting for Ali to show up, and while he waited, he wondered if he was doing the right thing.

Nigel knew that he had been an integral part of the destruction that had been dished out on the United States. He knew that Ali would be very happy with the work that he had done, but he couldn't help but feel a pinch of guilt as he tallied all the people who died because of him.

"Is this really what God wants?" Nigel wondered aloud.

Prior to converting to Islam, he had never been religious, but he could not ever remember God wanting to kill innocent people. It made him wonder if the God that the Christians worshipped was the same as the god that he worshiped in Allah. He never really looked into Islam before converting; he simply believed what Ali told him.

As he sat in his room, he wondered if he had made the right choice. "Am I truly doing the will of God?" Nigel asked himself.

Epilogue

Ali Basharat's car dropped him off in front of the United Nations building in New York City. He walked in through the main door and confidently strode up to the security checkpoint.

"Good morning, Ambassador," the security guard addressed Ali.

Ali was the Syrian ambassador to the United Nations. He had come to the United Nations for two reasons. One was to plead the case for more intervention by the United Nations on behalf of the Syrian government to help stop the country from being ravished by the rebels and the Islamic State. The other reason was to get guidance from his master.

Ali nodded to the guard and waved his credentials in front of the card reader. The machine was satisfied and displayed a green light, allowing Ali to proceed.

It had been a busy few weeks for Ali. He had been commuting between Detroit and New York via his private jet to ensure that all the attacks went off without a hitch. It was unfortunate that the vest house in Brooklyn was disrupted, but it turned out only to be a minor setback. The attacks on Washington, DC, had far exceeded his expectations. The United States government was thoroughly disrupted, though not yet defeated. Command and control of the United States military was uninterrupted, but a wave of concern had spread throughout the country. Months and years of planning had come to fruition with the execution of these attacks. There was more work to be done, but first, Ali needed to talk to his master.

Ali entered the private elevator that was reserved for diplomats and pressed the button for the sixth floor. After a moment, the elevator doors opened to a large vacant lobby. Ali exited the elevator and turned to his left. The room that he was looking for lay at the far end of the long hallway. All but one office on this floor were vacant so the two security guards who were placed outside that door weren't out of place. He strode up to the guard to his left and presented his identification. The guard received it and nodded to the guard on the right.

"Sir, you understand that we need to make sure that you are not carrying any weapons," the guard holding his ID said.

Ali nodded in affirmation, and the other guard began patting him down.

After they were satisfied, the guard returned his ID and opened the office door to room 66.

As the door opened, Ali felt small. The room was uncharacteristically large for the building, and the architecture was downright out of the place. It had an Old-English-library feel to it. The floors were dressed in a rare European maple wood and was stained and polished to a reflective shine. Ali could actually see the reflection of the walls extend downward onto the floor. The walls were dressed in mahogany from floor to ceiling. The far wall was almost completely glass and had a spectacular view of the East River.

There were a few chairs and couches throughout the room that seemed to be a comfortable place to read from the many books that were scattered throughout the room on various bookshelves. At a glance, it looked like there were a thousand or more books. The occupant of this office had once told him that there were actually about sixteen hundred. The vast majority of the books were either history or religious texts.

The last piece of furniture in this room was centered near the wall of glass. It was a desk that had been salvaged from Istanbul and dated back to the twelfth century. Upon entering the room, almost all visitors' eyes would be drawn in the direction of the desk, not to the desk, but to the man who sat behind it.

Ali's first stop, however, was at a small rug that lay only a few feet from the entrance of the room. It was a four-by- six rug that was used for Muslim prayers. Ali knelt down onto the rug and then laid out his hands in front of him. He moved to the ground in a bowing motion, eventually pressing his forehead to the ground. He held this position while waiting for his master to address him.

"Come," a solemn voice commanded.

This time, he could have only been on the rug for a few seconds, although in the past, he was forced to wait minutes; once, as long as an hour. Ali would never forget that day because it was the closest he had ever been to losing his life.

Ali raised himself to his feet and walked directly to the desk in front of him. The man behind the desk was tall and had the dark face of a man from Turkey. He had a strong chin and high cheekbones. His thick jet-dark hair was styled in the typical fashion of a worldly businessman or diplomat. He had broad shoulders and the physique of a man who worked out on a daily basis. Ali didn't know how old the man was, but he heard that he was in his late forties, even though he looked like a man in his mid-thirties. The only giveaway was the touch of gray that had popped up at his temples. The nameplate on the desk said that he was a deputy ambassador, but his rank at the United Nations meant nothing to Ali. Ali actually held a higher office, but his allegiance to this man was complete.

The man came out from behind the desk to greet Ali. He came up to Ali, grasped his shoulders, and greeted him in the ways of his native Turkey and Muslim culture. After the greeting was over, he motioned to Ali to sit on a chair that was placed in front of the desk. And then he strode around to his own chair behind the desk. "Ali, my brother," the man started, "you have made Allah proud. You have made me proud."

Ali felt a sense of pride, like a son would feel when praised by this father.

"Thank you, Mahdi!" Ali replied with a slight bow of his head.

THANK YOU

I would like to thank you for reading my book. I really hope that you enjoyed it. I did quite a bit of Bible research while writing this book and I continue to do so. It was my goal to create a story that God would be proud of. If you don't have a personal relationship with Jesus Christ, I would like you to consider starting one as soon as possible. I do believe that Jesus Christ will return soon. In my heart, I believe that it will happen during my lifetime. Obviously, I could be wrong, but it doesn't hurt to prepare yourself now.

> *"Then will appear the sign of the Son of Man in heaven. And then all the peoples of the earth will mourn when they see the Son of Man coming on the clouds of heaven, with power and great glory."* – Matthew 24:30

If you want to bring Jesus into your life, but you are not sure how, please contact me and I will try to guide you. Contact me at roadtorevelation13@gmail.com.

Reviews

If you liked this book, please find it in your heart to give me a 5-star review on Amazon and Goodreads.com. As an independently published author, reviews are very important to me.

Social Media

Please like and follow me on Social Media and check out my website.

Facebook:
https://www.facebook.com/TheRoadToRev
https://www.facebook.com/CliffWellmanAuthor

Twitter:
https://twitter.com/RoadRevelation

Instagram:
https://www.instagram.com/road2revelation

Websites:
http://www.TheRoadToRevelation.com
http://www.CliffWellman.com

CHARITY

When I began this journey, I decided that I would share my good fortune with others. The first book in The Road to Revelation series was dedicated to my father who lost his battle with cancer in the summer of 2016. It still pains me that he was never able to read the entire book. During the last days and weeks of his life, Hospice of Michigan was there for my father, mother, and the rest of our family. It would have been far more difficult to get through that trying time without them. Because of their service, I have decided to give the first 10% of revenue from The Road to Revelation series to charity. – *Leviticus 27-28-32*

Current charities include:
- Hospice of Michigan
- St. Jude Children's Research Hospital
- St. Vincent DePaul
- Put on the Cape: a Foundation for Hope (www.putonthecape.org)
- Northern Michigan Children's Assessment Center (www.nmcac4kids.org)
- The Key2Free (www.thekey2free.org)

In addition to these charities, my family has set up a scholarship in my father's name at the high school where he spent the majority of his teaching career.

I have been blessed by having an exceptional family and believe that we should help those in need. I encourage you to do the same. If you can't spare the money, maybe you can spare your time. Give locally and give often.

Thank you, again, for reading The Road to Revelation.

Recommended Reading

The Holy Bible (New International Version)

The Septuagint (1851 Translation by Sir Lancelot C. L. Brenton)

The Islamic Antichrist by Joel Richardson

The Mideast Beast by Joel Richardson

Mystery Babylon by Joel Richardson

Daniel Revisited by Mark Davidson

The Harbinger by Jonathan Cahn

The Mystery of the Shemitah by Jonathan Cahn

Revelation Deciphered by Nelson Walters

The Mark(s) of the Beast by Martin W. Sondermann